to: 'the one worth waiting for'
also lori, hayden, modesty, & my close friends.
nico, holden, asa, brennan, and
whomever else may come into my life.

THE ORPHANED
ANYTHING'S

THE ORPHANED ANYTHING'S

✦

memoir of a lesser known

A Novel

Stephen Christian

iUniverse, Inc.
New York Lincoln Shanghai

THE ORPHANED ANYTHING'S
memoir of a lesser known

Copyright © 2008 by stephen christian

iUniverse books may be ordered through booksellers or by contacting:

iUniverse
2021 Pine Lake Road, Suite 100
Lincoln, NE 68512
www.iuniverse.com
1-800-Authors (1-800-288-4677)

Because of the dynamic nature of the Internet, any Web addresses or links contained in this book may have changed since publication and may no longer be valid.

This is a work of fiction. All of the characters, names, incidents, organizations, and dialogue in this novel are either the products of the author's imagination or are used fictitiously.

ISBN: 978-0-595-47856-9 (pbk)
ISBN: 978-0-595-60044-1 (ebk)

Printed in the United States of America

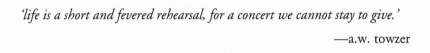

'life is a short and fevered rehearsal, for a concert we cannot stay to give.'

—a.w. towzer

NEW CHAPTER
stabbing my brother with the plastic blade from an osculating fan …
and other such thought provoking situations.

that's when i know i am near waking up. the abrupt indication appears to be when i roll onto my stomach, but i might as well get up … i know i'm just going to lay here, careen a couple of times, sway a few more, and then commence to think of all the things i should be doing instead of laying here.

i believe i am the only human alive to sleep in these bumbling lumbering phases. i understand now, after years of this sleep repetition, that i seem to have three, and these clumsy situation's only occur after the hours of thoughts that seem to run through my head without cease.

i cannot remember a time in my life where i did not have to have a mutiny over my thoughts or memories just to fall into what some might call sleep, but i simply call it a momentary 'at-ease of mental clamor'.

the first of my phase of my sleep cycle is that of the tent knees. aptly named, this is wear i lay on my back and my knees are bent, i thought as a kid it made my blue NFL knock off blanket look like a tent; hence, and ingeniously named, 'tent knees'.

The second phase is the discomfited fetal position, this happens only when, again, every thought has been explored and they finally concede to surrender until daybreak.

i have always wondered if there is a subconscious reason i sleep in the fetal position, am i trying to retrieve days in the womb; the safety or the silence? i understand that could be viewed as very odd, or @ very least neo-fruedian, but still.

never the less finally, when daybreak stabs like an unforgivable vengeance, i roll on my stomach, half laying on a pillow, and half uncomfortable. this is where i rattle in and out of consciousness and try to access what day it is, and what time i have to be somewhere, if anywhere.

laying here i realize i no longer need my alarm clock, i can't remember the last time i slept past nine a.m. but if i did have an alarm clock i would want to wake up to that one beach boys song 'wouldn't it be nice' (stereo mix) because i figure that song is so inconceivably happy that i could never again have a shitty day. the song is much to agitatingly happy. i want to say that i have a sleep disorder and seek help, but i know i don't and probably couldn't afford the medication even if one was diagnosed.

the last time i gave myself a prognosis it was not as much a disorder as an excuse really. i convinced everyone around me @ the time in middle school, and subsequently myself, that i had attention deficit disorder because i could not concentrate, or study.

but honestly who likes to study in middle school? TV or study? what 12 year old kid would rather do math over watching any given cartoon? with my new found hyperactive diagnosis i believed, simply because i felt like annoying my younger brother, that i had A.D.D. or A.D.H.D.

now i simply see the availability of ridlin as more of a glorified baby-sitter than anything else. parents are afraid their callow boys enjoy high energy activities a little to much (isn't that called childhood?). so they put them in a comatose coma by giving them a prescription drug to calm them down. thinking about it now i guess that's what television does, puts one in a comatose state … and subsequently baby-sits.

today like yesterday, i will chance away fate by foreseeing that it is is not going to be much different. i have to work my jejune job once again today and in a little while i will get up, enjoy my morning daily routine of addictions, and head out to carpe diem-ish. upon arriving to my tedious job i shall once again reflect on another morning in which i succeeded in failing away. then i expect to ponder arduously on all the items i didn't complete on my to-do checklist (a 'handy' notepad that my mother adorned me with complete with boxes to check and blank lines to fill in, *hence checklist).

i ponder between my irksome daily customers on what i should have accomplished in those early hours and once again vow upon all things i have justified holy that the next morning i will get them all done.

then i will tell myself the truth …

it will be the same as this morning.

i will probably just sleep in and let another day pass like the ceaseless traffic on I-5.

at first i was quite cynical about the whole checklist thing and sarcastically added to the list such items as;

[]1. breath (oxygen),
[]2. eat,
[]3. repeat steps 1 & 2 daily

    now i take i take it much more serious and have added such noteworthy items as;
[]1. find the cure of cancer and AIDS all in one easy to swallow pill
[]2. git smart
[]3. win the lottery

    still laying here upon my unyielding bed the sun glares relentlessly into my eyes. the air conditioner is out, i think i am starting to sweat. i never got the air fixed so i bought a base-minded rotating fan. damnit, i hate rotating fans. i mean really what is the point of it rotating? and to my utter joy and surprise the knob broke off so now it permanently rotates. someone tell me what is the point really of an oscillating fan? the fan, in essence, is playing with your emotions, its like AH! your cool for a second,
    now you are not,
    now you are,
    now you are not,
    now you are.
    i think i bought the dire ash gray fan more for the noise, in which i cannot sleep without anymore. i remember when my older brother and i were younger he used to fall asleep hours upon hours before me and immediately made this grovel/car-sputtering noise which irritated the piss out of me.
    so i begged my mother for a fan, thus my first addiction was established. i do not know which made me more upset—the onslaught of engine noises he emanated from his throat or the fact he was that kind of sleeper that he could fall asleep right away.
    i adored my older brother but have never come so close to killing someone with a plastic toy ninja sword, in our small closet-like bedroom, as i did on those exasperating night's. more than twice i plotted to disassemble the rotating fan and stab him with the plastic blade, or at least break off the knob in his throat. i never did.
    we were but kids and still i felt worried about everything around me, and always right when i tried to lay down for the night. i think most kids worried about if the boogie man or some other ominous monster loomed about in the

closet, or that they wouldn't be the first ones out to the tether ball court out @ the bus stop or worse ...

that the other kids at school would make fun of them for something they wore, said, or cultivated upon their face the night before; as was very popular in middle school.

as for me, i began to worry about little things from early on. @11 years old i was concerned about einstien's theory of energy remaining after death thus concluding the possibility of an afterlife, or if the cambrian era could honestly disprove darwin and the theory of evolution, or worse ...

what the kids at school would make fun of me for about the next day for what i will wear, will say, or for my newest edition to the family upon my face. i rarely got these beast's called 'pimples' but when i did they were so massive that once while trying to get into the movies the guy at the ticket window wanted to charge me double. one for me and one for my developed friend accompanying me.

so, it wasn't that bad. but in middle school it always felt that way.

i still remember, and to this day wonder if anyone else had ever done this; when i was a kid we lived in a two story house and each night before bed my brothers would always send me upstairs first. i would pretend like i was not scared of going up the old unnatural rickety stairs by myself. so on my way up the haunted stairs, and right before i got to the top i would say in my deepest voice;

"ok, i've got the whole place surrounded, come out with your hands up." and upon doing so pretend to call for backup in my imaginary walkie-talkie, complete with the static induced 'kkkkucccccct' sound at the end of each sentence.

i did all this because for some reason i always thought that some escaped convict, or spawn of satan phantasm, was hiding out upstairs and might truly believe and fear that the whole place was really surrounded by the local police force.

the enigma is that being 11 the low tonal

"ok, i've got the whole place surrounded," probably sounded more like a pre-pubescent mickey mouse after a helium balloon than any one on the local police force, ever.

hopefully.

nevertheless i still find myself to this day calling for backup when exploring new dark places @ night by myself, complete with 'kkkkucccccct' static.

now it seems to me that when i wake up i am usually pondering the same nonsense that i fall asleep thinking about. my thoughts are much deeper, like did i shut the garage? do i have to work tomorrow? do i have an STD?

you know ... deeper.

so here i sit, on the side of my bed with all three phases of sleep in my near past, and my blankets distraught around the bedpost as if i was pedaling an exercise bike in my dream. is it so bad to look forward to sleeping the next night?

lately i don't want to be awake at all, my head feel's bludgeoned and i can actually feel the muscles in my enfeebled pale arms getting weaker. i would attempt a pushup but that would require some sort of energy, and motivation.

a "im up, what more do you want from me?" sticker hideously controls the back of my door, and i always tell myself to tear it down. my roommate/awarded older brother put it on there as a joke, but now i view it as one of those inspirational-quotes that major corporations hang on their employees cubical thinking that it is honestly going to inspire after the second day.

perhaps it sum's up the extent to which i am motivated. "im alive, what more do you want from me world?"

it's a glorious and underrated mantra regardless.

NEW CHAPTER
overanalyzing is the wine in which dreamers are drunk

the day starts with coffee, ends with coffee, revolves around coffee, no joke. i work at a local coffee shop called the 'bauhaus', located at 301 e. pine street in seattle, wa (in case you ever want to come in and introduce yourself). at first i thought it would be advantageous to work where i would be surrounded by psuedo-intelectuals like myself and we could discuss deep and unexplored topics, feed off each others liberalness, and completely figure out the meaning of life, religion, lust, and thermodynamics.

in no particular order.

understandably a reasonable goal, or so i thought. we could debate all this while meeting interesting customers, who would enlighten us on depac chopre's teaching and the inner workings of aeronautics, and all of this while baristaring their desire for a 16 oz. split & skinny mocha on ice.

now struck by catharsis, i see in retrospect it was an idea much like communism; simply idealistic, but not feasible. and don't get mocha on ice because you don't get the piece of chocolate like you do when its served hot, and it doesn't taste as good to be honest.

it pays the rent, well not really, the last of my student loans are paying the rent. but i am proud of my associates degree from community college. (insert note of sarcasm here)

i plan to go on, i really do, but @ 24 year's old i tell myself that i need to ever so cliché-ly 'follow my dreams', (editor: imply that i have dreams though i do not) college will always be here but youth won't. i make sure to tell myself that each and every day, so future regrets are based on good intended past philosophy's.

what good is an AA diploma anyway? it can't get you anymore jobs then a high school diploma, so why do community colleges feel the need to give them out? its like saying "good, but not good enough".

in all honesty they should hand out applications to state schools at the gradua-
tion ceremonies and not those empty diploma holders. i don't even know where
my AA diploma is, honestly it is probably in some box in my mother's attic, or
lost.

who cares, its not like the bauhaus coffee shoppe hired me on my educational
achievement's and a 15 page essay on "how coffee has changed the face of north
american economic and financial community forever". they obviously hired me
for my handsome face, my firm thighs and abdominal muscles, my louis vuittion
man-bag, and my ability to make every customer smile with satisfaction and idol
chatter.

or not.

(im on a role with this whole sarcasm stuff)

if they gave me a raise for every day i came in with a darker bag under my eye,
or a new wrinkle accompanying the corner of my cornea's, i would be well, i
wouldn't be struggling for rent. my boss was concerned for awhile that i was on
heroin. i wish that were so, it appears a drug addiction receives more sympathy
than aging not so gracefully and the incessant lack of sleep.

addictions: well me working at a coffee shop is moronic. that's like asking a
struggling drug addict if he wants to work unsupervised for the downtown police
department labeling drug bust evidence in their narcotics department. or better
yet, asking the alcohol anonymous meeting to reconvene @ the cha cha, our local
tavern.

with coffee, i drink just about as much as i sell.

here's one for you,

and one for me,

one for you

et cetra …

here is a profile of my stereotypical customers; they come into the coffee shop
with a man bag and journal, he/she wears the black rimmed glasses to look like he
is ready to study for a test he/she doesn't have.

they bring in their novel, like the "the good earth" by pearl s. buck. which they
have read to page 10 but have been reading it for about 3 months now; though
they have read enough to know all the characters names in case someone of the
opposite sex shows somewhat of an interest in either him or his book. he/she
probably got the book from one of their college dorm roommates who actually
read it, but for an extra credit assignment.

their journal is the first thing they break out, (they don't really write in it but have it out for dramatic effect). they honestly begin their addiction to coffee like most scene kids begin to smoke, simply to look the part.

ok, i'm not going to lie, that's my life in a lame but honest nutshell. i'm about half way through the good earth and don't like the character lotus at all, and i swear that the book is mine.

all this contributed to my quest to work for such an establishment, but in spite of my grand delusions of psuedo-anything it is clear that i am simply working here to people watch and my insatiable heroin-like-fix to small brown crushed beans, that keeps me employed here.

Kosacov, Ayden employee number 143-1983
Sunday, September 12, 1pm-7 pm

damnit, im here 2 hours early, could have … well i couldn't have slept more, but still. i could be filling out college applications, or beginning to start on the novel 'war and peace', or more importantly in the grand scheme of life—watching absolutely nothing on television.

sometimes i wonder if anyone else notices this phenomenon. the worst programming on television is on sunday mornings. i guess the networks figure that everyone has a hangover, or are yelling @ their kids to get ready for church. or both. so networks air all their handy dandy new fast automatic infomercial or re-cancelled shows which jumped the shark in 1976.

TV is the biggest colossal waste of time. everyone does it, no one admits to it. how many hour's have been wasted in a rigamortis state,

no one in the room talking.

everyone bored.

silent.

wishing their lives were a little more like the character on television and less like their own.

life.

lived.

vicarious.

there may be nothing worse in life than showing up to any job early, you sit around waiting to work. its not as if i can take the bus back home. the $1.15 (X's 2 to get back) ride (calculated by cost per month for the bus divided by trips to bauhaus), and 22 minute 43 second ride here would not be worth it just to get back home just to watch chef lung wang try to sell me ginseng knives, or other such prodigious products.

"early?" brian the shift manager questioned.

('yes you overzealous slave driver, i want to prove to you and the rest of the staff that i want to be here early to be the best employee bauhaus incorporated has ever had, do you have an employee manual handy?

because i have only memorized up to page 31 and left my copy at home on the night stand where i read it 3 times a day like a koran!')

-i thought all to myself dripping with inner brilliant dialog.

"i didn't know if you guys might need help a little early, it being sunday afternoon at all." i said, knowing full well sunday afternoons are about as slow as an afternoon special on lifetime.

"thanks, but no. its the end of the month and i am already over our allotted hours. corporate's really coming down."

what does that actually mean? ill never understand their manager lingo, as if they would really be upset about the $13.90 minus $1.87 for taxes and social security that bauhaus would honestly 'lose'.

here is where i go into detail about my friendship with brian the shift manager.

we do not have one.

he is not an important character in this book, but i added the conversation bit in because i felt that the inner dialog needed a rest.

i love this coffee shop ever since the first time i steeped foot into this place. when you walk through the broad and iron gate doors you walk right into the antique looking oak counter which sits about chest high and displays the local bakers delicacies. don't be fooled, some of them are day's old, but some how all taste decent.

behind the counter hangs a small wooden sign, engraved most likely by a thoughtful customer, but is out of sight from patrons. it reads,

"without a doubt i have you. surely I see you. thinking is the wine in which dreamers are drunk, i know. but sometimes i'd like to be dreamed of too. when you are like that in your book, all evening, sunk."

(-Victor Hugo—words in the shadow.)

i see the sign every day and have thus come to the conclusion that it is utterly true, "thinking is the wine in which dreamers are drunk ..."

introspective, autobiographical, "to really know thyself" (aristotle) ...

all goals, but for me, never seemed a reality.

solitary seems so elegant to the outside. but for the forgotten our heavyhearted world doesn't call it solitude, we call it loneliness.

i have heard it said that it is during these moments when your heart can finally hurt, it's in these moments when the music life composes can finally move you. it's these second's when dreams are dreamt, and suddenly realized. but i think it's in these moments that i wish i were perpetually intoxicated with more than just isolation & the thought's that eminent from the mind of a insubstantial recluse.

i hate that victor fellow. the only reason i have thought all the way through his quote is because i have hours to stand at the register. staring, thinking, spacing, bored.

in my opinion the best seats here at the bauhaus are actually the bar stools to the right as you walk. this is because the building has such high ceilings and half of the structure is made of glass, thus looking out to oversee my resplendent city of seattle is a sight to behold in the morning over coffee, and 'the scene,' a local zine/paper.

the wood here is warn and fatigued in some areas, but it only adds to the ambiance of this place. it is a continual cluster of persons, as there is never a time where a customer is not in line, and to some extent that makes time at work speed along well … expedite. the entire block is on one of the many scenic hills in this town so on a clear day you can see for kilometers around. there is a giant photograph of some creepy father figure fellow named walter that stares at you when you walk in the door. i can't tell if he is saying 'your late' or 'where have you been?' with his body language. both expressions seem oddly applicable to me every time i walk in the door.

i feel as though in some way i am feeding into a subculture that has birthed out of this city. im not speaking of the 1990's movement but of an independent, leave me alone, 'i know more about what's really going on in the world so i am better than you' movement.

i just don't think our generation has anything @ all to unite us, for instance; from the late 30's to the 40's the western world united for a worthy cause of fighting dictatorship and world domination fighting in world war II. if you didn't fight as a young person, you were making bomb's.

the 50's saw one of the greatest generations in american history, with a hard-working country the youth of the america clung to a thriving postwar economy, the beginning of the civil rights movement, and the rat pack.

60's and 70's protesting united a generation of noisome hippies who believed in free sex, experimentation with unknown and untested chemicals, unbathed sanitation habits, and really formidable music.

80's saw youth unite under the best music ever in what could possibly the worst dressed era in the american/uk youth. but ever since the 90's it seems we really have nothing to unite us, we have nothing to bring us together and fight for a common goal or dream.

we need a common hobby. we should all collect stamps or coins, or something. we need to go and get ourselves into a real war, just so we can be pissed at the government. we won't listen to the fact's, and even if they are telling the truth lets plot together that their wrong and claim them as lies. i just want to hold a sign, i really don't care what it says. i want to stand out stand on a street and yell at passing cars, "what do we want?!!, when do we want it?"

in all honesty i don't care what i get and when i get it, i just care that im standing next to someone who cares that i care. but until i can protest inevitable whatever's there will always be the bauhaus.

upon your arrival to the bauhaus you will notice that the entire left hand of the store is abundant with books, which are all used, tattered, and for sale. i have concluded the books are on the location not because any of the owners of the store or myself are well read, but to resonate an aura of knowledge.

i honestly cannot tell you the last time we sold one of those books, but it adds to the feel this place is trying to delineate. the random titles are none that you would have heard of. even the authors of these book's are unrecognizable. i believe someone must have bought these books @ a library closing because they still have the place to stamp the date in the front of the book. classy.

on the back left wall, as you walk up the stair's to the frank loyd wright-esce upstairs there is a bulletin board filled with random opportunities; such as yoga in the mountains, painting or guitar lessons. 'wanted bass player for an alt-country/ godspeed you black emperor band.'

standing behind brian the shift manager was my on and off-weekend hookup, though that's completely one sided, im always on and she's more or less the off. she's a fairly attractive girl with a larger nose, smaller breasts, and as of late i have noticed she always appears sweaty or oily, especially on her back and especially when she wears those spaghetti strap type shirts.

i have psychologically diagnosed her, and my expert advice is that she has an old maid/senior year college instinct that makes girls long for a non-superficial, committed, high hoped of someday tying the knot relationship. i have deducted this because she is consistently quoting and rambling off the list of all her friends that are getting married.

she tends to have this way of always saying "us" and "we" when in conversations with other people on our infrequent happenings. every time she mention's 'us' it kind of hits me the wrong way, in a repulsive i never want to see your face again way.

i hate when she, or any girl for that matter, says "love ya" because you don't know if she says that to everyone of if she is trying to get you to say "i love you too", thus pushing the level of the relationship to an all time newly awkward level.

"you will never guess what happened this weekend," jenn-iveve the perky but small breasted/randomly oily barista said.

"what?" i asked knowing i didn't really want to know.

"do you remember my friend shai? the one i would bring in when i was going to college this past summer? well anyway she met this guy at that club neighbor's of all places, and get this … he just asked her to marry her!!! can you believe it?"

*monotone

"no. no i can't"

"that makes like 14,000 of my friends that are doing the M."

"wow im really sorry to hear that." i said under my voice in sympathy for her not being one of those 14,000 and for the couples getting married.

"what?"

"i said wow, i am really happy for them."

"what did you do this weekend?" jenn-iveve the perky but small breasted/make out friend said.

"same old" i said ('same old' sounds better than completing the old line "same old, same old" i always thought).

"you should have called; cody, brandy alexander and i all went out to some house party, holden showed up and played a couple songs here and there all night long, it was pretty epic!" jenn-iveve the perky but … said.

"cool"

"i had a lot of things i had to get done saturday morning and it really took care of my weekend jenn-iveve."

"like what?"

think, think, what was saturday? make up …

"well im co-planning a show in portland in mid—november and had a photo shoot all day with some friends" … saying portland so it would be about a three hour drive from here, saying november because hopefully she would forget by then, and saying friend because i enjoy thinking i would like to put that on my to-day list to acquire one someday.

"what was her name?" she asked.

"why do you think it was a girl?"

"well you said you were with a friend all day and i just thought."
"it wasn't, his name was" think think "nick" (after nick cave)
"nick who?"
damnit
"nick seed, he's also from portland" knowing portland was about 3 hours away ...
"cool"
"yea"
"well ..."
"yea i just came in early to pick up my paycheck and go deposit it but i guess there arrant here"
"they always come on tuesday"
"yea well, i didn't pick mine up from last week"
"ok"
"yea well, i think you have a customer"
"ok"

we will have a one way meaningless sleep over tonight. i will want to go farther, and she will want some type of verbal commitment in return. voices will raise, i will hold her and tell her it's ok simply so i can try again.

if you know your an asshole and you admit it, does that make you less of an asshole?

relationships in the male/female sense of the word have been an enigma for the past, well, all century's. how many thousands of books have been published on the inter workings behind a cohabitation ritual.

i must admit though, i do think that women have evolved much more effectively than men. there cerebral cortex are much more compatible and have much less interference when interacting with one side of the brain to the other. men are far, far less complicated.

while hanging out with a girl a male companion could ask, 'hey, what are you thinking about?' the women could repeatedly reassure you that nothing is on her mind, but after the 13th attempt she would break down and unload on a comment the male companion made weeks ago.

however, if a female asked a male companion 'what's on your mind?' and a guy replied that nothing is on his mind then trust him! there is absolutely nothing on his mind. if you could look at a picture of his mind at that instant it would be like a tv screen turned into channel 85, the one that is just static at 5 am.

we are just not that complicated to figure out. for instance while looking in the periodic section of a local book seller i noticed that on the top of one of the men's magazine's i noticed the heading said, "women, money, beer, gadgets, car's & more." i thought to myself what a horrible stereotype of men that was! how insulting it was that you could sum up the whole existence of men with those few surface words.

i got a subscription.

NEW CHAPTER
romance & love are such illogical topic's when talked about in less than 30 degree weather.

where to go with two hours before work ... there is either the used book store or bar24/7 that has nothing good on the menu except beer. which at 11:14 on a sunday a.m. sounds a little taboo.

i always wondered about 24 hour places like this bar/grill and such. like who at 4:49 AM is going to a 24 hour strip club? what is the point? i want to meet the man who at 3:48 AM wakes up out of a dead slumber, and instead of getting a midnight snack, or rolling over into the fetal position, decides that seeing tassels swung in a circle in his face sounds like a more feasible alternative to REM. who needs a beer at 11:15 AM? maybe i am naive or just not yet an alcoholic.

i love used book stores, i love the scent of decomposing books, or is it the decomposing feeble ladies who inevitably work at places like these. i think on the applications to these places there are only two checkboxes at top and you have to check one or the other or your application is automatically disregarded. i have a suspicion that the application looks something like this ...

*********BOOKWORMS APPLICATION**********
THANK YOU FOR YOUR INTREATS AT WORKING AT BOOK-WORMS, PLEASE FILL OUT THIS APPLICATION AND TURN IT INTO THE FRONT DESK.

1.   ARE YOU A ... (PLEASE CHECK ONLY ONE)

{} disgruntled x-librarian with black-rimmed glasses
or
{} saggy, overeager, & over makeup'ed grandmother

*if you currently fit neither category please stop filling application out now. thank you,

-mngt.

but my favorite part of the used book store is the fact that the books are used. i love to read a book that someone else has previously owned and underlined all their favorite passages. if they have written in the columns the book is worth double its weight, its like not only do you read what the author is saying but what the other reader is feeling.

i have always wanted to track down these other readers, like look them up in the phone book just to see what they are like. not out of a stalking sort of way, but just to do it for self gratification. like a cia agent, kgb … whatever. i just want to see if there a shut in like myself.

its amazing to me to read philosophy books because people are always trying to object to what the author is saying as if they have added something that this particular philosopher has never even thought of.

religious books are also amazing, for instance once i bought an old copy of the talmud, the jewish holy book, just to read what the previous owner had underlined. i figured this guy has already read this whole thing and underlined the best scenes in the jewish peoples history; therefore i cut all the slow parts, like the 1,344 chapter's of lineage's, and just hit the theatrical and action scenes. it doesn't get much better than fast food religion.

sometimes i make up stories in my head about the previous owner of the book, was he/she tall or short. maybe they were millionaires or maybe they lived on the streets and their only solaces was in a paperback novel. are they alive or is this book the remnant of what the children threw away or donated the local goodwill/salvation army when they passed away. either way im fascinated by every new book i purchase.

true story though; i once met this guy on the street one day and at first he asked me if i wanted a guided tour of the city for only 24 dollars, i promptly explained that i lived here in town. after we talked for a a couple of minutes i noticed that there were a couple books on the table and i questioned him as to whom they belonged to. armed with stereotypes i assumed he had accumulated them through petty theft or found in a cardboard box behind the local bookstore.

he explained to me that they were his and then went on to tell me that he was an ex-heroin addict that had dropped out of high school and was trying to make up for lost time by reading every book that penguin publishing had ever came out with.

now i don't know how many penguin books have come out over the years but there must be literally thousands. i wouldn't have believed this particular fellow but he showed me his plastic bag and all that was in there was a towel, a water bottle, and about 12 other books.

after he schooled me in every other book ever written i was pretty convinced that this methadone patient knew more about literature than anyone in any high school, and on top of that probably any community college graduate.

his name started with a 'j' i believe, and if he gets a chance to read this memoir know that i think you have made up for lost time and that i'm proud of you for owning up to your mistakes and being a father to your 9 year old daughter.

back to this aged book store; you see i come in here all the time but this lady never remembers me, i swear she is either a robot or she has her entire monolog memorized, it always goes something like this.

"good afternoon young man" says the lady who never remembers me.

"hello mam"

"have you read anything good lately?"

now at first i was honest when she would ask me this question, but realizing she has no long term memory i soon began altering my answers.

"yes mam, actually i just finished 'sunny day real estate' by elvis costello."

"oh lovely, i've only heard of that book but never read it. do i like reading? yes, why yes i really do! so i will have to get to that someday."

"great"

"do i have a lot of time to read? no, i am busy and really must work, if there is anything you need help finding young man just let me know."

"great thanks".

then it hit me, every time we talk she asks herself questions and then proceeds to answer them herself. how bizarre.

i have heard that the most intellectual people spend quite some time talking to themselves, but it comes off peculiarly lonely to me.

it never hit me that she does that until today. i question whether i have some annoying idiosyncrasies and no one i come in contact with has bothered to apprise me about it. i wonder if she has done that for years, and/or if any of her friends in the ex-librararian circle of friends ever picked up on that.

sometimes i wonder if i am the only person who ever thinks in particular thoughts. does anyone else think like i do? i am sure there are, i wonder when original thought ceased? who was the last person to come up with a maiden thought?

i feel so sporadic, like my mind is 14 places other than where i am right this second. i remember a couple of months ago i read this poem called 'anywhere out of the world' by charles baudelaire, and he was talking about how our lives are like being in a hospital bed and how everyone thinks they would be happier if rolled someplace else.

"life is a hospital where each patient is possessed by the desire to change beds. this one would like to suffer facing the stove, that one believes that he would be cured next to the window. it seems to me that i would always be well where i am not, and this question of moving is one that i will discuss endlessly with my soul."

did he read my mind? everywhere is my hospital bed. i move here/there and i think someone somewhere else is finding ecstasy elsewhere. contentment evades me like the women of my dreams, like fame, like money, like power, like intellectual stimulation. chicago has art, london has music, new orleans has mystery, paris has culture, spain has elegance, new york has trend, and my apartment has ... only me.

the poem continuously reminded me of that saying "the grass is always greener ..."

thinking of which, do you ever wonder who coined the phrase 'the grass is always greener on the other side' because he or she should be rich off mechanical royalties by now because so many people use the phrase so very nonchalant.

its so true, the phrase that is. i think the guy who came up with it said it because he was happily married at one point and then this hot young woman that his best friend had been dating made a pass at him at a party one night. of course he turned her down but after a year of getting to know her and secretly fantasizing about her when he made love to his wife he broke down at an office party the following year. he was so drunk he just made out with her because his marriage was getting boring and because he had made her out to be everything his wife was not. when in all reality he only liked her because she actually was interested in what he had to say, and she was something new to screw around with (the theory of strange).

ended up they got caught at the party by some of his coworkers, his wife divorced him, his best friend never talked to him again, and the girl he committed adultery with turned out to be a transvestite. after he was fired it was rumored that he went crazy and lived on the streets for years, and his final statement to the court @ the custody trial was "the grass always looks greener on the other side."

everyone @ the court house that day liked the saying and started telling everyone they knew. and thus it spread.

i am pretty positive that's how it happened.

or how i imagine it happening anyway.

insert theory of strange: i think that millions of years ago in the ice age men had to try to impregnate as many women as they could because they wanted their genetics to continue and the species of human being's to survive. fast forward 2000 years. nothings changed. its not that we feel that our girlfriends/wives are not as good as the people that we cheat on them with (because you are just exchanging one problem for another set of problems) but its just....

well ...

their strange. they are something that we have not explored. they are not as smart as you, and they don't even have to be as good looking as you. we just want something different to fall asleep to. were trying this thing you call monogamy, but for pete's sake even a women came up with the word. really.

*ok, so i don't know if that's true.

but wouldn't that be weird?

"you want to come over tonight?" jenn-iveve asked ardently when i got back to work.

"yea, well i work till 7, so after that ill stop by. what did you have in mind"

"i don't know hang out, movie"

i think we have established 'movie' as our code word for disregarding the video rental and each others previous moral boundaries.

but there comes a time in every mans life when he has to step up and become a man of integrity and pursue intimacy, thus building a stable relationship. and when he knows that she is not the girl he could see himself marrying then honorably he should swiftly, but gracefully, bow out.

this was not that time.

"sure." i said thinking that i have never had a time like that.

fast forward several ommisble hours.

walking home at what feels like subzero temperature i replay the events over and over of the last few omissible hours. but unforgettably it was forgettable. another round of miscommunication. she thought i liked her because she "could feel how much i cared (about her) when i touched her so gently" but in all reality i just wanted to touch her. but my sensitive side came out sounding like this ...

"yea sure, whatever."

she didn't take that as a sweet nothing, but that was as romantic as i wanted to be with her. thus walking home in this fall seattle night, especially when you were counting on not going home at all, was especially cold. as for my situation tonight, it is like they used to say 'all's well that end's.'

honestly i don't understand the rousing of romance all that well. I used to believe in this thing called fate, or destiny. a romantic romeo and juliet, monte and veronica, etc. but now I feel a little jaded, maybe agnostic to the idea.

but choice used to seem so unromantic, as if some mystic force was not behind the meeting of 2 beautiful individuals. But now I think choice is the greater of the two simply for this fact: by choosing someone you are saying that out of all the people in the entire world I have decided that I want you apart of my life in perpetuum, for the rest of my life, and no one else.

no haphazard circumstance, no chance meetings where distant planets align … it ss simply two rational individuals who make a choice and an effort to remain together.

for years now i have convinced myself that choice is the better of the two. but now I want to believe in fate, that there is someone out there created with me in mind and vice versa. but both seem like mythology, or star wars; simply an anecdote to reality. how did they all stay together?

for me after the initial phase of "strange", new, and exciting wear's off i seem to lose interest. i think i need to marry someone who is a makeup artist/or a hair stylist, that way every couple weeks she looks different. maybe a psychologist, so at least she will change for the better every so often. i don't know what that means. i don't even know what im saying now, its a long way home and i am trying to think of anything but this wintry night.

romance & love are such illogical topic's when thought about in less than 30 degree weather. it should be saved for unpedantic discussions on the eiffle tower, or long walks on an endless beach resort commercial. i have no first hand experience on the motif of love. discussing love for me is like lighting a lucky strike underwater, reason less. who really knows what love is? it is like the wind, or God, we have never seen either but we know that they (hopefully) exist. it is the cause for many broken hearts, and yet boundless completeness.

I think it is amazing that the english language is one of the only language's that has a sole word for "love". I envisage it is a word that is overly battered in our society. how can you tell your dad/mom/relative that you love them, and then within the same hour say "i love your new clothing", or "don't you just love that album?". are we not stating that this thought/feeling called love can be attributed to both someone we deeply care about and also a resplendent looking inanimate object?

many songs have been written about this experience called love, but in the words of christian winterset "i love you means more if first said tomorrow."

in other words don't throw the phrase "i love you" around haphazardly like it will return to you when you truly need it to mean something. i think people should wait until they have observed the 'behind the scenes', and made sure the other person has truly proven that they are not a mere actor/actress. for if "all the world is a stage", then love & lust are the inspiration for each and every individual performance.

NEW CHAPTER
f this place sick.
… no seriously

today: its really early, thoughts begin to take over asudden, i want to roll back upon my side and try to sleep even just a little more. please, a little more. 5 more minutes mom. think think. it must be around 6 AM. its monday i think, yes, its monday and my only day off.

a quote by sir thomas browne has been echoing without cease from ear to ear all last night, and subsequently pounced on me the second i awoke. i can't remember but i think i read it on a wall somewhere, or one of those quote books people memorize to spout off at family gatherings to look astute and brainy.

"your time here on earth is but a small parenthesis in eternity."

i don't know if he was trying to be motivational when he said that, but for me it makes me feel like crap. a nothing. in light of the entire galaxy i will be unavailing in the orphanage of this universe and ineffectual in the face of time. that guys a jackass.

why is it that we as human beings feel that we need to make our mark on this universe anyway? how many other billions of people have walked upon this earth and thought the same things i have. i wonder if anyone will remember me in the years to come, i wonder if i am in any way monumental.

The fact is i am not. within hours i will be forgotten to some degree, a rock upon my head will tell of a year, and a name, and maybe a bible verse my spouse liked. it will not tell of the emotions, the accomplishments, the love (if any), the tragedy, the picture's, the songs, the failures, or the children i might leave behind. but why do we want a legacy? what makes us long to be remembered? i am yet to figure that out.

i contemplated on write several book's, maybe words on a piece of paper will encourage someone to remember my name, or speak highly of me when i am gone. but paper decomposes and the interesting thoughts i once had will soon be outdated, and any new theory i embark on will then be old, and tossed away by a new idea or concept, radically overturning mine.

i could write music, but as is the nature of the beast it will someday not be the current radio felicity, and will be forgotten … i know my music would only be of the current trend, and not timeless like i would hope. maybe my best bet is to have several male children, all with my last name. and i will start a family tree … of course a few generations along i will be a name and a number on a tree … and somewhere a rock.

a tree and a rock … that is what my life will be narrowed to in about 100 years.

i recently began to research my ancestry online. i did one of those searches after coming across a blinking advertising and came up with a potential lineage and meaning for my last name and such. since not a lot of records were kept in the eastern europe my line goes back a few generations and disappears. my dad thinks ghengis kahn came in from mongolia and raped his foremothers and that's why we have the squinty eyes. well that's what he said.

but after hours of this research, and my eyes dry from the computer screen i began to wonder why it was that i was so intrigued by the names and dates of those i would never meet or ever really know anything about. i determined that it is because stories of our past seems to linger within us a sense of collective immortality. when studying our immediate families chronicles there is some sense of foundation and belonging especially when we link ourselves to history and the past. we want some sense of family, and every time the page would scroll back i wished i saw the word 'king' or 'prince' kosacov, just so i knew that somewhere in my families past someone mattered to somebody.

but then it dawned on me, as if i were awoken from deep sleep by gunshots to the stomach … we want to study our ancestors in hopes that one day we will be studied as intently, or even more intently, by the generations of decedents that we are going to leave behind.

i remember buying one of those 'all about my grandparents,' book at a bookstore and giving it to my grandmother for christmas. i couldn't imagine why on earth, years later, i found that book on her shelf untouched with not so much as her name written in the front. i couldn't understand it because i so long my grand kids to give me that book, sit down, and allow me to recount stories of my middling life.

so here it is monday morning, 6:13 am on my day off and this is what i have to mull over. my legacy. i'm pathetic. i find working weekends is acceptable to me because it fills the need to find something to do or hang out somewhere. that way if anyone asks what i was doing/or did that weekend i can tell the truth by explaining that i had to work, and not have to tell them the unfeigned truth that "even if i didn't have to work i am a social outcast." the 3 females i have ever dated in my life (which includes my 5th grade romance from mrs. adams class) are girls that came on to me. the only pickup line i have ever used (unsuccessfully) was "oh my god, i am so sorry, i hope that doesn't stain. ill go get some napkins."

i hang out in coffee shops and libraries because
A. i may work there
B. its the only place i can sit alone and not have to explain why i i am doing so. i am sure it is assumed by guilty bystanders that i spend the majority of time with my online friends chatting to people that i will never meet, about experiences i will never encounter.
and they are probably right.
C. all the above
but that is why i like computers; because everyone is everything they want to be there. the boys are men, the perverts are perverted, the women are men, the men are women, the middle school girls are teenagers, the high school girls are in college, the college girls are women, and the women can lie and say they have the bodies they had in college. the lonely are brave, and i can have weight lifting and sexual encounters. people are dating and breaking up with lovers they have never even seen! how is this not astonishing? this is an amazing technological age we live in my friends.

private chats, and threats from 30 year olds who weigh less than 120 pounds. its magnificent. i sign on, and today im a hero, tomorrow ill pretend i broke both my arms or something so juliacampo22 will send me a get well email card. random i know. but dillusionary friends are still friends.

so the day off. i think today ill go follow my dreams. (again please note cynicism in previous sentence.) i really did have a dream—once, or do, or work on it in my spare time (which is all my time). i am an artist, at least that's what i used to call myself to get girls, but has never helped. still do call myself an artiste every november so my mom will lay off when the microwavable dinner thanksgiving day questionnaire is issued out around the banquet table. these disconcerted questions are always served right after the turkey but before dessert and always include the soul searching ...

"so what are you doing with your life nowadays?"

i started out painting. i had huge dreams that i would move to some amazing loft apartment near capital hill, i would paint all day, magnificent works, blaring radiohead, screwing all night. i would never talk, and wear all black, and people would question if i was a vampire or just artsy. i would only drink wine, which i would acquire a taste for and not have my cheeks real from the bitter taste. the wine would be from some ancient of days but amazing year, (like 1998 or something). my pieces would go for thousands and thousands of dollars for originals. even the prints would be so rare and priceless that people would have to go to auctions just to glimpse @ one. i would stroll down the streets of new york city and someone would be selling matted rip offs of my high art, i would flip over there tables and burn my fakes right in front of them.

at the end of my life i would go down next to monet, du champ, maybe even di vinci as masters. i wouldn't die but evaporate into thin air, thousands would morn and i would be written down in history as a man of mystery. my great great grandchildren wouldn't even have to search their ancestry online or in reference libraries because my name would be mentioned with pride at every family gathering.

i have no idea where this is going.

i cant paint.

i cant so much as draw.

the extent of any talented art as such was some half coherent stick figures in a sunset and birds that can be created by drawing the letter 'm'.

im not remotely creative with acrylic or oil whatsoever.

jackson pollock was my inspiration. a canvas on the floor and i would splatter stuff and affix objects to the canvas and write catchy slogans on them like

"what is art?" or "i am artsy" aptly implying self-righteous sarcasm because honestly i knew what i had just painted was no were near art. clearly aware that the dada movement was over and i was judged and left wanting as a virtuoso.

that is when i took a photography class and began snapping pictures of everything, and everyone.

i remember when after i told my mom about my new found passion she exclaimed;

"i do not understand why photographers get awards and money for the pictures they take, God made it all. you don't see or hear about God getting any recognition for those beautiful landscapes and people."

thanks, really mom, that's great. just when i wanted a moment of exhortation from the women who birthed me, she turns it into an insipid and underappreciated touch of a button.

what do you say to that?

'Mom, there is no God, he is a figment of a societies imagination used to push rules and regulations those in leadership wish to establish. god is basically the opium of the people and a tool of those in power.'

for some reason i do not think she would go for that particular line of thought. needless to say i pursued photography and got somewhat decent in doing so, winning ribbons from here and there, even the owner of the coffee shop let me hang some on the wall at the coffee shop. (wow, ansel adams here i come ...)

* sarcasm is down to a chemical formula.

i love it though, especially black and white, there is just so much feeling that can be evoked by a piece of paper, and thin layers of ink. the light, the texture, over or under exposure, sharpness, brightness, contrast, saturation, temperature, tint, shutter speed, the type of lens, et cetra.

the dark room is one of my favorite places to be in this world. especially if you come late @ night when everyone else is out doing what college kids do, and only myself and a few stragglers who have procrastinated remain. much like being in an elevator it is presumed that the dark room remain silent. i don't know who began the tradition of elevator's & dark rooms, but i appreciate them. to get away from it all jesus had the wilderness, buddha went on walks and sat under trees, jim morrison had whisky, william s. borough had acid, and i have the dark room. if isolation is the furnace of transformation, i could be ashes by now.

i love how each piece of equipment i own is like a paintbrush or easel. i could bring out the cracks in peoples faces, or evoke youth by just a simple adjustment or different angle of light. i love older people, i love to look at how unique each of us are. like we were planned.

like we belonged. as if we are different but at the end of the day were all the same, with qualities we each shared but never copied.

my favorite picture that i have ever taken was of an older man in an over coat, his brimmed hat he kept stingily pressed against his chest, as if it were a family heirloom in wartime. he paced the local museum as if something new was going to reappear at the wall he had just visited. i snapped a profile shot of him staring with his mouth agape at a small statue set into the floor. it looks like he is shocked by the art piece, but in reality he was just yawning. the whole thing was in black in white except for the piece of artwork behind him, which is in color. it brings out the old mans silhouette perfectly. sure it looks amateur but i am new at this and it is the best i have done so far. i am not as creative as i would like to be, i can't manipulate my environment like the great's can, i simply sit back and snap a whole bunch of shots and hope one or two turn out.

i have done one art show downtown in which one piece was bought, by my younger brother, asa. a lot of people commented but no one saw the need for random people, or deteriorating objects hanging on their wall. i guess that would be a little awkward to have a picture of someone you have never met hanging in your hallway or over the mantle, or even worse in your bathroom where they would stare at you through the course of events that took place in that particular room.

maybe i should change to nature, everyone likes mountains and pieces of wood, with green leaves.

i like dying people, and abandoned something's.

i believe all's well that end's.

i do not like nature all that much to be honest, give me concrete, or disintegrating statues, or a rusty something.

orphaned anything's.

i once had the ingenious idea to make a coffee/table book of graffiti i found on bathroom stalls and back stage area's of local venues. though the book would be a graphic novel per se, it would be hilarious. like drawings of wretchedly drawn naked women, truck stop humor, idiotic racist remarks, %$#@ someone for some reason, or for a good time call _____.

my favorite bathroom stall philosophy that i have to date taken a picture of was in a truck stop right outside tulsa, oklahoma in which it read;

"f this place sick"

it didn't even complete the curse word. it was just that and i never really figured out what that meant but for some time after that it was my favorite phrase, i would say it after most everything.

"ayden are you going to turn in your journal assignment? your really falling behind in this class,"

"are you coming to work?"

"do you want to sell your soul?"

all could be answered with a swift

"F this place sicK!"

nothing came of the coffee book, where do you begin to market something like that?

but i still have the pictures.

photography is an expensive hobby, and again that is where student loans comes in. i need to sign up for classes in the winter simply because i cannot afford not to. who cares what grades i make, i just think that you have more student loan money that you are allotted to take out if your a junior. and that brings on a whole new assortment of brightly colored problems such as, how and when am i going to pay those back? i know, after i defer the loans as long as i can, ill tell the company that i have died in a horrible accident including a razor blade, dental floss, a car bumper, some heroin, and a bright yellow forklift. i think they really wouldn't raise to many questions and drop the loans.

honestly though, i did that.

no, seriously i had just turned 18 and saw some karate movie and thought this is it! im going to be a kung fu guy and take lessons and beat up ralph machio and stuff. so i signed up for lessons but told the guy i would be moving soon and i might have to cancel the contract. he mumbled some stuff, but really i just don't think i was paying attention to what he said, i just wanted the uniform and belt, and to start breaking some boards. months later i got kind of tired of doing roe tae kwon do and turned in my uniform and stopped going. a couple of months later i started getting these notices in the mail about how i still had to pay because i signed a 3 year contract. talk about sleepless nights, i had no idea where i was going to get 70$ a month from. so i called mr. roe and told him i had to move, and he said that he couldn't transfer my account, and that he didn't do collections or something like that. i tried to reason with him and the collections agency but they just didn't seem to care that i was bored of tae kwon do and wanted to quit.

months later after they started calling my house and my mom started questioning me i finally called the collection company and in my deepest voice i told the collection agency that ayden kosacov had died. they expressed their sympathy but then went on that they needed a death certificate to close the account. well that got them to stop calling, but my credit rating is shot all to …, but who cares i'm dead right?

ohhh, F that place sick.

NEW CHAPTER
moral relativism
is my personal absolute.

when i was a kid i had such a fascination with anything paramilitary. it wasn't just the typical boy/guns/gi joe phase that all little boys went through. i know this because it stuck with me through middle school, and seeped into my high school days.

i would get a group of my neighborhood friends and we would go into the woods behind my suburban sprawled neighborhood and play war. i even went to west point military academy and met with an advisor because i really thought i wanted to be an officer in the military. imagine that me, of all people telling troops what to do, and preparing tactics to kill other people. and here is the most embarrassing part of this all, i actually was in army rotc in my 7th grade year. it wasn't so bad the first week, but then i was issued this atrocious green uniform and forced to wear it once a week. i would always hide out before school and change my uniform between first and second period. i finally dropped out of army rotc because the girl i had a thing for in band class, karen elkhart, saw me before school and kind of held a smile back when she saw me. and it wasn't one of those flirt smiles, it was more like i can't believe your such a dork smile's.

my lord, i can't believe that i was such a dunce; band class, rotc, choir, i mean honestly i think i had a vendetta out on my own social life. i should have gone out for flag core and finished myself off!

in retrospect i don't think it was the guns or hand grenades that drew me toward pursuing the career in the military, it was the brotherhood of the troops that i saw in every movie, magazine article, and book that i had saw/read. i never really felt apart of something. i never really felt i had a close knit family life so the idea that there was someone out there that had my back and i had theirs in the face of adversity was authentically attractive. i think that is why street gangs are so attracting to so many young males. if they had no family life, the feeling no one cares, the hope that you belong, for life or death—you have a place with a gang.

the gang colors: camo. our mission: impracticable. our backgrounds: diverse. our future: unpromising. it seemed in the constant face of death many walls were dropped without one word spoken. and i wanted those real friendships, i wanted to look back and have stories of bravery, honor, and a tattoo which represented people and places i would never forget.

i wanted to fight for something, i wanted to stand for a cause. i want to believe in anything. i wanted to deem something worthy to die for. looking at what i just wrote in this paragraph i see i was searching for a religion and not so much a career in a governmental war machine.

i think were all searching for something. i wonder if anyone has found it. i wonder if its different things for different people. i can't say i have ever met anyone who was complete. everyone wants something else. maybe that is why buddhism is such a popular thought invading western culture, because everyone wants what he has ... and i do not believe it is enlightenment that they seek. i believe its the fact that he claimed he did not desire anything more than what he had. he said he killed desire and thus he was supposedly content. but as westerners i don't think we could ever be content with what we have. our advertising, commercials, television shows, revolve around the curiosity of something more, new, and shiny. never to be satisfied. our right to the pursuit of happiness is a farce because it is never-ending, much like the galaxy, or like me running the mile in gym class. pursuit of happiness is a lie because what makes us happy today will be out of style tomorrow.

school. education. middle school. high school. why do all these words conjure bad connotations?

The most confusing, lonely, forlorn years of my life are glorified as "the best years of my life" as one of my high school teachers put it. Was she insane? She must have had a better high school experience than I did, I remember sitting in class after she said that scared, and pissed. "if its all downhill from here i am screwed."

i would skip every high school pep rally, just straight up walk out of school; i got caught but there was no way i was going to spring testosterone fest 01.' i had the school spirit of a corpse, honestly i can't even tell you what our school colors were. but i can tell you that our mascot was the fighting salmon. were they serious? how tough is that? hey, opposing team, were going to flop around in your hands for awhile, then try to swim upstream, and that should teach you to mess with us.

the entire school thought i was on something. i guess because i never kept my head up, had no friends, and did very few drugs.

while taking senior pictures with the entire class i pretended to put my fingers, in the shape of a gun, in my mouth to show my gratitude for the 4 years of education i had received. the principal caught me and yelled for me to leave. i guess he thought i was flicking off the camera, when in all actuality i was trying to splatter my brains on the people behind me. never the less all the kids yelled and made fun of me, and actually was a little stoked because i didn't even know they knew my name! even if my last name isn't faggot, @ least they knew what my first name was.

it feels like one day i walked into kindergarten, and the next i walked out of my high school. life is so all of a sudden, and then its gone. sometimes the only one's i have to hold on to permanently are not people at all, but memories of those people.

like scott silcox, 3rd grade, mrs. osbornes class. he was more hyperactive than i was, if that was possible. he was shorter than i, and that i remember. we got along because no one else got along with us. we were always in trouble and most likely in trouble together. i remember randomly that we both liked rap music probably because our older brothers did. scott showed me that sitting in the back of the bus was to the advantage for ungovernable boys like ourselves. i moved to the other side of the country shortly after 5th grade, and thus never heard or saw him again.

soloman koontz. we were both 13 years old, and he lived outside the city limits. i remember that he lived in a undersized trailer, but his home was like an colossal empire of activity's. we built forts, burnt action figures in epic battles, and even swear to this day that skeletor almost came out of the fire at us. we talked of girls as if we knew what we were talking about, or actually talked to any of them. we would go camping, and he taught me about the outdoors, and still to this day those inculpable recollections were some of my favorite memories. he pursued art, then girls, then mind altering substances, we have lost contact altogether. last I heard he was a trace dj in orlando, florida somewhere.

heath seabolt, 7-10th grade, taught me to sing (or an attempt at singing), or at least harmonize because his voice was so incredible. he was the envy of the every kid at church including myself. i never felt I could match up, or even come close, it seemed he had it all, the looks, the singing, the pastors daughter. while playing capture the flag i swear to this day that we saw a moving object way up in the sky go very slow … then turn do a 180 quite quickly, then turn back around and soar past us so swift. we believed in UFO's … at least for the next week. he was a good friend, that much i will never forget. i wanted so badly to date or just have the nerve to talk to his older sister. he taught me that life isn't about what you do or look like, its who you are. i didn't believe him. part of me still doesn't. he went on to pursue music, eventually getting signed to a major label, i went off to community college. we talk occasionally when he comes into the coffee shop on break from his world voyage's.

john bervard, 11th grade. he was a certified cowboy-hick, or as certified as you could be being as that we were from the 'backwoods' of seattle. my trend was that of a punk rock kid, we were an oddly peculiar pair but as random as it seemed we would work out to be really good friends. working at the pizza lodge has a way of humbling people and bringing them together for a common task. that task being one of hard work, determination, perspicacity, and the keen ability to avoid insanity through the monotonous hours making fast food.

we became close friends after he put his used dip into my mom's x-boss's barbecue pizza the night after he fired her for no reason. he was a little more vengeful than I, and he taught me that I shouldn't let people walk on me. he also taught me that there is a whole culture underneath a hood, and 'there's nothing a little duck tape couldn't fix'. he joined the military, got married and we've lost contact for several years now.

melissa borders, first year of community college, i had the distinct privilege of breaking up her engagement to some pervert. sure i thought she was attractive and an amazing artist but even more attractive is the fact that I could make her see that there are better people out there than that prostitute she called a fiancé'. call me a home wrecker but I prefer a quasi-super hero with an overactive savior complex. we dated, it didn't work out on a theological level, you see she thought for herself.

she taught me that who oneself is makes all the difference in the world, and that no matter how much we want to change the other person in our romantic lives the essence of human beings should be to stay true to oneself. She was an astonishing artist and once drew me a picture of marilyn monroe that must have taken hours upon hours. last I heard she was engaged to another guy who was "amazing" and treated her "soooo well". I have no idea where in this world she is, and most likely will never see her again.

its amazing how we are the composite of everyone we have ever met. it appears to me as of late that we are interwoven with people. The belief system of every man is an island to ourselves is clearly that of a man who justified his own self-righteous actions and did not want to have his conscience bothered by those lives he was going to inevitably destroy.

i do not think we could come up with any belief system on our own. someone had to tell you and me about it. i chose to accept it or reject it. I believe in nature and nurture, but in some context i wonder if we were left alone our entire lives what would we believe in? how would we explain the sun and moon?

i think if left all up to me i would have concluded that the earth was in fact flat, and that the sun revolved around this flat earth, and the moon is made of cheese. ricotta cheese. we know because we have been told, we are told because someone believed, they believed what they saw. i have never seen, yet i believe.

we are nurtured by parents, peers, mentors, and even people we play with as children; all these teach and speak into our lives more than we may ever admit or think about.

sometimes i wonder if i were brought up in a buddhist home would i be buddhist? if i were brought up in a hindu home would i be hindu? i wish sometimes i had a clean slate of religion, philosophy, theology, (etc.) just so i could see what i would come up with on my own. how much of what i know did i adopt from my parents and those my parents allowed me to be surrounded with? am i me, or a mirror of everyone that i have encountered. are they me, and i am them, and ..., oh hell.

what an endless senseless circle i make everything.

im 24, a sophomore here past community college, and it feels like all these kids her are so much farther along than i am . they seem to come straight out of high school on their daddy's bank account, or smart, or just not A.D.D. i know secretly they are just there to show me up with their youth and brains. some sort of cosmos conspiracy theory. there seriously out to get me. each and every one of them. its simple blitheness to pretend i have paranoia.

i am in no way looking forward to university. not so much because of the harder classes, but the simple fact i hate fraternity or sorority anything. if i am ever desperate enough that i have to buy my friends by joining alpha masta beta anything is the day when suicide is imperative and no longer an option.

when i finally go to university ill take night classes, ill wear all black and tell everyone i have loft.

ill make up some story like i have been in europe backpacking or following my dreams these last few years. both being a lie.

what have i been doing these past few years?

nothing.

soul searching isn't true. i gave up on God when my dad gave up on me. he took me to sunday school and left with the choir director, i am now comfortably numb to anything tied to the word "religion".

searching truth isn't true, every moral instilled in my youth has now vanished. truth is relative, and what may be good for me may not be good for anyone else. i will tell my fellow classmates that 'we are all an island to ourselves.'

i know the entire above paragraph is all bullshit but it expands the possibilities for extending the borders of my moral conscience.

moral relativism is my personal absolute.

in other words i am now at an all time low where i am capable of justifying just about anything i want to do.

and lastly; searching wisdom and knowledge isn't true either. i think i had more figured out in when i was 19 then i do now. all i know is that i don't know anything at all. and that's a start, right?

so what have i been doing with myself?

eating, sleeping, existing, living, being, taking up space, inanimate, mostly dying, merely living, limbo.

i believe it was blaise pascal who once said

"be comforted; it is not from yourself that you must expect it, but on the contrary you must expect it by expecting nothing from yourself."

i honestly don't know what this quote means but it felt comforting to not expect anything of myself, and pretending to do it out of a philosophical decision than admitting my own lack of self-confidence is exhilarating. the fact incompetence can be justified is proof my own little sad world is a meddling failure.

NEW CHAPTER
i'm a nonconformist ...
just like everyone else.

when walking downtown here in the evening i intermittently look around at all these people with their armani suits, and the women with there channel handbags and matching scarves and wonder why they were so lucky to be born with everything figured out. they just look like they know what they are doing. if they have any insecurities at all it has been masked by there flawless makeup, acting lessons, smiles, and grappling yet prestigious hand shakes. how do they get their teeth so white, how did they get success as a genetic predisposition, have they read some timeworn text that i have not yet ascertained? did they figure out who moved the cheese and why and did they get it back?

they look so ... found.

and i feel so ... opposite.

does money make one gratified? have i missed my calling? we have all heard the saying that money doesn't make a person happy but @ this point in life i have no money and i'm not happy. i am totally willing to try the whole rich thing. i could be a guinea pig to prove or disprove the previous asinine theory.

at times i believe that if i don't get enough zeros behind my bank account statement that my family, this society, our populace, and that girl in the lingerie advertising will never be pleased with my life. why is money the mark of success? when did passion and desire become replaced with economic and financial wisdom as the chief character trait desired in a potential life companion? will my spouse never feel secure if i don't obtain? hence and therefore eliminating possibilities of a nostalgic future, with a memory laden past.

the western world is consumed with consuming!

we are rich in material possessions but poor in quantity of time.

will i never afford a car that goes 0 to 60 in whatever number is the fastest? will i never have a white picket fence? will my 2.5 kids hate me for raising them in a home where we reverie love and loyalty over stocks and bonds?

my only reassurance in all this is my confusing self inflicted lie that i am a nonconformist, and money would never make me satisfied. i wear my hair like a mop because 'i don't care what you think of me', i wear these clothes because your not, i sell where as you bought in. i know who che is, my shoes don't color coordinate with my shirt, on purpose. i have read the communist manifesto, and wrote in it's margins, i don't pay taxes ... voluntarily.

i am a nonconformist, just like everyone else.

(underline that last phrase for the next person who buys this book at the used book store, write a little something in the column like "wow, that is simply abysmal!" or "i could paint that into my jackson pollock knockoff art piece right next to the 'what is art' logo".)

we are bombarded with the subliminal message of conformity everyday. you should find the statistic on how much advertising a person sees before they graduate high school. i don't remember off hand how much it was, but i remember thinking "man that's a big number." advertising is everywhere, on billboards and movies, newspapers, magazines, sides of trucks, i have even seen people tattoo logo's on their arms. we have become who we think we need to be, and not who we want to be.

advertising agency's are simply creating needs and wants where none previously existed.

what do we really need?

what do we really want?

and what are the differences between the two?

i have come to the realization that we all purchase out of fear, were afraid were not good enough, or pretty enough, or in or of the latest fashion. we purchase the most modern trends so that others (who we don't know) will find us socially acceptable.

i have decided to buy products because i like them instead of trying to impress people i don't.

... but in my case i think i need to start buying "stuff" because Lord knows i can't impress them with my life.

i don't want to sound like a freakin hippy, but i sincerely believe simplicity is the answer, and i hope over time i can become more of a minimalist.

why are we so attached to our possessions?

do we control our possessions or do our possessions control us?

i think we should buy gadgets/possession's for their usefulness rather than it's status. think about it, we buy out of fear that we are not going to make the right impression. if you walked into a business meeting with a .75 cent coffee from the convenient store you might think that you are making a bad impression on your clients. but if you brought in the same tasting coffee, made in the same part of the world, but this time bought from a corporate coffee couture with a smiling mermaid on the side than its acceptable. odd really. but it's true. and it doesn't go for just coffee.

what is the use of any other car than the one you have that runs? are you honestly going to use that much more space on your computer that you need the latest? does your old coat not keep you warm anymore?

human beings make no sense sometimes if you really think about it. odd really. we are all the same processed & packaged conformists, just like everyone else.

NEW CHAPTER
this addling skating rink called life

the usual addictions in the morn which include brushing my teeth, putting in my contacts (i have horrible vision), deodorant on special occasions, and finally a shower.

a shower is not just water affected by gravitational force falling upon my pale skinned naked body: it is more like a spiritual cleansing, or an amazing grace salvation experience, and silent confession is held every morning.

i've noticed that after the most conniving or wretched moments of my life i take long, long, long, showers. as if the hydrogen and oxygen mixture is suddenly empowered by the great spirit of the american indians, or a burst of catholic renewal itself, it turns to holy water straight from popes house in rome, or vishnu, or mohammed or whatever, and in essence cleanses me.

it doesn't work, but for the moments i am in there i am at peace with, well, heaven, hot water, hell, and a razor blade against my cheek. that guy from last night has gone down the drain, and thus i am a new creation.

after i shower i stare in the mirror for a while, seeing if there is anything new, not being able to remember what i looked like the time before, as if i have always had these small cracks near my eyes (my mother calls them 'laugh lines' as if that makes me feel better about them) and bags under my eyes. my pale skin seems to glow in this light and i wonder if other people will notice that i missed several places while shaving in the shower.

i wonder if anyone will care, i know now i don't.

then i realize if i do go out today it will probably be to go return a video, or to shoot some pictures of who knows what. if i am lucky i may find a bathroom stall that is untapped with some fresh hate filled or perverted graffiti.

wow, what a staggering life.

mine is the only life i know where the only adrenaline rush is a bathroom stall, and a shot of caffeine that coarse through my veins. i wonder if i can put espresso in my veins, i wonder where i could get clean needles this time of day.

god, i am pathetic.

today i should walk, i used to be into health, or just a pe class or 2 in high school, but i never had this gut that seems to leak frantically over my favorite pair of jeans. of course i have had these jeans for about 2 years now.

i never really got into trends or style, probably because i could never really fit into any of them and if i could i couldn't afford them.

its always amusing how people get stuck into the best years of their lives. like the old guy who still has his graying marine buzz hair cut because the best days of their lives where when they got home from 'the war'. or the guy who still thinks the mullet looks 'radical,' because his 'good ole days' were during the period of iroc's and the ever adroit pet rock.

my glory days must have been some time ago, because iv'e realized i haven't changed my clothing tastes in about 8 years. only once can i remember ever being truly enamored with an item of clothing.

i think i was in the 5th grade, my father's job took us everywhere around the united states, I never really had a place to call home until we moved here to seat-tle later down in life. but this story takes place right after we had just moved to irmo, south carolina and I had met neighbor friends who were around me and my older brother's age. they invited us to go skating @ "skaters choice"; a local roller skate rink where frequent all night skates were exercised. my parents allowed my brother and i to attend one of these such affair's, so on a friday night we left home, with enough money to rent skates, but not enough for speed skates.

it is amazing how over time our perception of something so inconsiderable as fashion, or heavy as self-esteem or self-worth seem to adapt to how other people view us. we slowly evolve into the words and actions of others pushed upon us in our young lives. we are like a moldable clay, slowly being built by family and peers; the concrete-words that chisel-our self-confidence. but I marched to my own drummer in irmo that night.

skating to the beasty boys "you've got to fight for your right …" i felt that i had not yet in my life fought for the right to party, and i was going to start that night. i didn't know where the party was, and even if i did i probably wouldn't have been invited. there i was skating in my brown rental skates in a never ending circle. tan short short's that made a cheer leading skirt look like an amish norm. my shirt was a royal blue button down with 2 parrots on the back which i indi-vidually named that night, but currently don't remember. my hair was that of a mother cut military issue right out of boot camp, and probably the brunt of sev-eral jokes that night from un-adoring equals, but as for me, i was "fighting for the right". at that point in my life i had been home schooled for a year or so, and the concept of "in" or "out" meant nothing to me; the word's trend and cool had no bearing in my life, but i soon learned. the hardest way. the heartless way.

i recall the names chosen to sum up my existence in grade school, i still remember them even now. they are actually comical to me now; heavy laden ayden, fat face, chubs, etc. but back then it battered me every day to get up and go to school. i used to pretend i had a knee injury just so i wouldn't have to play the given sport of the day in physical education class. i figured i was going to be the final kid picked again, and i did not need the daily re-solidification of my place in this life; last.

i often wonder why we spend so much of our lives caring about what other people, that we may never see again, think? but we do, and such is life. well, my life. as my high school pope morrissey once said "why do i give valuable time to those i would rather kick in the eye."

i can only try to be myself, and not what any one else in this addling skating rink called life wants me to be. if i could find another parrot shirt i would buy it. i would then name the two parrots on the back, wear really short tan shorts, hit "skaters choice", and fight for my right to do something. i am not sure what just yet.

but be warned, i will fight.

NEW CHAPTER
it's either love, goodbye, or death
when slow music is in the background of a movie.

i take my timeworn rolleiflex automat 35c camera and head out into the oncoming breeze, through the city, and towards the cobalt blue water. the wind makes the amber red and incandescent yellow trees around me clamor with an almost orchestrated rhythm.

when i was a kid i used to pretend that God spoke to me in the wind, i rationalized it all by saying i can't see love, i can't see God, i can't see the wind, so they must all be related right? when i was young and afraid that God wasn't listening to me i would ask God for a sign and sometimes i believed that God pushed air across my face to prove he was there.

i never got the love part of my equation. i still am entranced by the wind, its just God and love that i don't really or really understand.

love.
i thought she would be here by now.
as if the gentlemen known as love had a time piece.
i wonder if he walks the street in solitaire, also.
i know he does not*
for if he did he would understand the lament in my heart,
and would be here, at least by now.
what if he is with his lover, by a fire.
she is reading to him, listening to vinyl
(an orchestra i presume, or at least something of mood).
he is busy. in love.
or maybe he is tired.
maybe i should not bother him,
he has had a long day at work and we all know love is manual labor.
he has clocked out working several jobs and is expected in kiev tomorrow.
i'd better not disturb him.

maybe he has bad vision.
maybe he is near sighted and i am not the flamboyant type.
well im must inquire as to an appointment for him
or a more boisterous shirt for myself.
maybe he is a she. yes!
and she has fallen madly in love with me and is searching the god's
for a way to become mortal,
and we will live out our romance in the south of france for eternity.
oh how suddenly am i in love with love!
i now realize i am only in love, with love.

i should really send that in to readers digest or something of that caliber.

now that i have my newfangled bag strapped on and my camera in hand, i have to evaluate which cd's fit my disposition best and take off. it seems i religiously listen to my cd player on the bus to work. i pretend that i am in a movie and the music in my headphones is actually the soundtrack that the audience can hear. but today i am walking across town, i need to listen to something slow, soothing, so the audience knows that something amazing is about to happen. (if you want to listen to what i am presuming would be great music for the background for the next scene in my imaginary movie, please listen to the band called 'the sea and cake.' more specifically to a song called 'the sporting life', it's perfectly deliberate)

you see its either love, goodbye, or death when slow music is in the background of the movie.

i should walk across town in slow motion, glancing to a fro, walking with purpose, waving good-day to old acquaintances, and helping a poor elderly women across a busy intersection, save the day, then pick up a scarf that the exquisite young attractive girl walking in front of me has precariously dropped. i bend down to pick up her light weight cashmere scarf and she turns around, she is gorgeous, and suddenly now so am i (where did this six pack come from?). we stare into each others eyes, mouths agape (all still in slow motion of course). she asks if i want to go and get a drink and i reply;

"why? your beauty is intoxicating enough"

we grasp each other as though lovers for all time, and cry, and make love all right there on the street.

"this is what forever feels like" i whisper in her ear,
and whatever.

there was an old lady though, she didn't want me to help her across the street. i think she thought i was about to mug her or something. there was no day to save, and there were pretty girls but none dropped their scarves, even if they did i would have probably tripped on it, tripping them in return and breaking my arm and their legs. there would have been lawsuits, and i would have been charged with assault and battery, and they would find in my bag that cd that i stole 3 years ago from a used store and would be sentenced to death for use of air that could have been used for the children with bright futures program. they would learn that i ran over 2 squirrels in my moms car in 1 night. i am watergate, and vietnam, and worldwide poverty all rolled into one awkwardly pudgy barista.

and all by midday.

NEW CHAPTER
i don't care that i am
going to die someday,
its the fact no one is going to care that scares me.

i spent the afternoon wondering around, looking at this doable city of mine. the reason i love it is that its big, but not overbearing or overwhelming. on the outside, sure we have skyscrapers, but once your here its really quite inactive, especially on a monday afternoon. its getting to be fall, my favorite season of the year. everything changing, everything dying. it looks like the trees are on fire, fading and burnished maroons.

i always wondered what the world would look like if i had created the universe. would we think pink clouds are weird, because in my world they would all be pink., like they look when the sun is setting. the sky would be more violet than anything. in other words the sky would constantly look like a sunrise or sunset. none of this half ass blue sky, yellow sun, and white clouds crap.

well whoever or whatever created this place did a really good job with these particular trees, with the wind blowing it makes for some miraculous pictures ... that no one will buy. but whatever i love them, and @ the end of the day its my opinion i have to sleep with. alone.

i take pictures of anything dissonant or abased looking. i don't know why i love things in chaos, disorder, or decaying. its life, its the summation of hope, eventual decay.

i love abandon buildings and widowed cars.

forsaken any things.

where do i hope to take this photography stuff anyway? i mean i plan on graduating with a degree in it, but then what? all those people with photography degrees end up doing one thing. weddings. honestly i wonder if that is not a cruel joke played by the worlds mythological gods.

this is a conversation between the greek god charles to his right hand demigod weird goat-beard boy bruce:

"ok, when we create ayden make him so he masters and loves to paint and draw, well versed and creative in all types of mediums in art. no scratch that make him love art but no good at it. then help him find photography but not love. then we will make him predisposition to failed relationships but then make his career at.... weddings!! (laughter all around).

just watching him develop others happiness in a dark room while tears crash down his cheeks will be my favorite part! we have to tell aphrodite and demigod paul about this one. we could make an entire mini series/reality show up here. we will get hours of laughter and amazing ratings all at the same time. and if the ratings start to drop just give him some prescription drugs and little vodka, he will take it from there."

i promise i am not on anything.

what is it about decay, rust, and death that i find so entrancing, honestly. is it because it is the last and final unexplored adventure or option for all mankind? i am not sure, but for me its just that every funeral that i have ever gone to it seems as though they are so peaceful. no smiles, no furrowed brows of dissatisfaction, just contentment stapled on their face. that's what i want. there are two times in life one does not have any concerns, worries, or responsibilities;
in infancy and death.

death.
i don't care that i am going to die someday, its the fact no one is going to care that scares me.
i try not to think about it to much, i figure i might as well get out all i can out of this life while i still am alive. though there was a time there for awhile that i made several drafts of suicide notes, each one including outlines of what i want at my funeral. but then i had the catharsis that i was sincerely writing them for real and it kind of snapped me out of it.
but do you want to know why i decided not to kill myself?
because honestly;

1. there wasn't a lot to say about me at the service and i didn't want some priest to make up some jargon about how i was this or that just to make my life seem somewhat productive or worthwhile to society.

2. there was not a lot of accomplishments that could be mentioned at the service and i wanted to work on that.

3. and most importantly, i made a list of all the possible people that might attend my funeral and honestly the total number of participants (including the priest) came to the staggering number of nine.

i don't want to go out like that, i want my mom and brothers to think that i had friends, and a secret life that they never knew about, in which i was massively popular. i wanted a community, any community, to come out in droves to support my withering mother (who would appear to be drowning in her own massacre) and my brothers, who now actually showed emotion and were pounding on my casket with their fists ... tears splattering off my dark amber coffin because they never told me how they really felt.

"oh god ayden, why, why, we loved you so much and were so sorry that we never told you how much you meant to us. we loved you more than anyone in this world and definitely more than that one girl we hooked up with last weekend at that one party, (was that last week or the week before. we don't remember honestly.) regardless you inspired us to be who we are today. why, why God, why couldn't you save him! why didn't we see this coming?" and they would both say all of this in unison of course, screaming at the top of their lungs.

but i have no friends.

and am not quite sure my mom would even cry. maybe for dramatic effect of something, or because she saw some star in people magazine doing it at a funeral for another star.

my brothers are quite busy and quite egocentric to pound on anything.

here is an example of one of those suicide notes that i dug up from the bottom of my 'writings folder' found in the bottom of my disheveled desk.

(i think all suicide notes have or need to start with the key words DEAR, CRUEL, & WORLD its just required.)

dear painful and unusually cruel world,
you suck.

i was lonely and you never wanted to meet me.

that's cool though, at least i sold a piece of art at one of my shows, and made the best damn latte you ever had. i should really leave that last part out.

to my brothers; you can have what's left of my motorcycle, it runs it just needs a new cylinder. i think they are like 49.00 online, you might want to check around for something cheaper.

to my mom; my books and journals, please read some of them if you want to learn something about me.

to salvation army; my camera, no one else will want to use it my family.

to my dad, nothing.

there is nothing after death. except a content look super glued upon my decomposing (but perfectly makeup'ed) body.

sorry mom, its just the truth.

goodbye,

ayden blaise ransom kosacov.

ok, so it was more of a pseudo-will/suicide note, but still. it was sad that i had no tales of great explorations, or achievements of any kind that i could remember to write down to remind people of how important i was. thus i am still alive.

and now you know my full name. ayden blaise ransom kosacov.

yea, i know. awkward.

here is that dysfunctional story, and one more reason to hate my dad. so he loved reading psychological journals, and the self help section of every sunday paper insert. i guess he read somewhere that when a child has a unique name he begins to identify with his own unique nature, and thus becoming individualistic, and encouraging creativity, confidence, and overall genius. what it ended up doing is making my life in grade school hell! when other kids were writing

john smith

i was misspelling

ayden blasze ransome kosachikov.

dear god, the other kids had such an easy time with their names. they got finished with their assignments so fast and then they got to go to the reading room with all the other kids with short unoriginal names and those amazing bean bags. and while i watched through the glass at their good times and fortunes, i was still at my desk striving to be creative, confident, and an overall genius.

but being that i was the second born my eldest brother got it worse. really i swear ... and he is about as unoriginal and stale as the love child of an aging politician and c-span, addicted to downers.

if i am ever a parent, which would mean i would have to have sex with a willing subject so, yea, i wont be a parent,—but if i were! i would name my boy bob and my girl sue, with no middle names, and change our last name to "jones" or "smith," that way they could get the good bean bag chair and read all they want while the others struggled to be original. i just pray that i am a better father to my kids than my dad.

NEW CHAPTER
"the sun will come out chin tiger."

i do not really honestly remember much about him, my dad that is. every time i do recall a memory or such i try to repress it, oh i know its wrong, but its one less thing to concern myself with. the only thing that i remember him saying to me directly was when i was 11 or so.

"hey ayden, what's your favorite baseball team?"

what? baseball? think think

"uhh ... i like texas"

"texas huh, more like tex-ass this year!"

he got a chuckle out of it, though i did not understand how that was funny. i had never heard him curse before so i think that is why the memory is so vivid and has stuck with me all these years, after all we were a church going family then. and baseball? i never liked baseball, texas just happened to be the biggest state i recalled at the moment, therefore hoping that it had a team. if he had asked me specifically what team i liked in texas i think it would have blown my cover because i would have said something like "the bandits", "the cowboys", or the "tumbleweeds" because that's the only thing i thought sounded like a name for a sports team in texas. it was like word association and i passed, found not being a psycho or ignorant or something of the sort by my father.

he cheated on my mom. i never got his side of the story, he says there is one. and maybe there is, this family holds on to more secrets than the cold war kgb. i just didn't want to hear it, tuned out his tirads in court, and never took his calls. he never seemed to fight to hard for custody or visitation, and the only time he came to see me during high school was really just a side note to his business trips.

i honestly never really put much effort to get to know him i couldn't see the point. @ first we would go to his place every other weekend, but that faded away when us brothers watched tv or played outside by ourselves and left him out. i was young but i remember just feeling uncomfortable & unwieldy around him, all the time.

the ignoble divorce happened so suddenly and so very odd as well, it was as if he wanted to put a double edged knife in my moms heart. he sent the divorce papers on february 14th, and he made it abundantly clear that he wanted the papers to be delivered on that day specifically, or so the courier said. that was the day he didn't come home.

he booked tickets for 2 to denver and poof he (they) were gone. what could my mother have possibly done to him that she deserved so many knives thrust turbulently in her back. ill never forgive him for that.

she masks the pain, or maybe she is over it, or maybe she cheated on him first with a family friend or maybe mic jagger, or something crazy like that. maybe she is a pole dancer and all these years she has been working at that 24 hour strip club @ 3-5:59AM and he just found out about it. or maybe it was because they constantly fought about money, and where it went, and why it went there, and "really where did it go?".

maybe she always knew he was cheating on her with the choir director but was dillusionary, thinking that she could change his mind. thinking that he really did love her deep down, but he didn't. at least i don't think he did. he said "i love you" once in awhile but it was like "love ya" or sincerely yours, at the end of a letter.

always stated, but never meant.

monday night.
here at the apartment. i am bored of the computer. no one really on line to make fun of. no liberals complaining about the failure of the reganomics era. no right wing christian coalition member complaining about the rights of the unborn child. no pervert trying to see how young i am. boring.

i'm bored of the television, nothing on except shows that i've seen and feel i could do a better job of producing. there's always the hitler channel (formally history channel, i think all they do is talk about world war II, and maybe that's because they don't have any video footage of any war prior: or they have some sick obsession). there is always music television channels, which i believe is more interested in selling meaningless and trendy products to minors than showing relevant bands or decent music videos.

tomorrow's tuesday, big day of work in which i pick up my paycheck that is already pretty much gone. i have my share of the water, electricity, and rent due. i need to save. but for what? need to start to 'budget' but i want to develop this film in my camera.

the worst expense besides development in photography is the frame for me. no one wants to buy a picture without a frame. it could be an prodigious parker young or loretta lux print worth hundreds but without a frame its not only not bought, but not even looked at.

i want to get a better job, but know i am too lazy to look for one. i want a better life for that matter, but i'm to lethargic for it to matter to me. i am bored and feel that i have explored everything that i will ever explore. i have learned, not all, but all that i feel i am going to apply myself to learn. i have not made love, but i've had sex, meaningless yes, but i get the general idea.

i've experimented with substances, there's no feeling that i will trick my mind and body into feeling that i have not already smoked, snorted, or shot.

ok so not shot, im scared as hell of needles but i added that in because it makes me sound tough, like sid vicious in a chelsea hotel or something. what else is there. my roommate has a gun collection, maybe i should go to a shooting range and fire a couple off at targets that look like people in case someone tries to break in our post-gheto apartment, or america gets invaded by sri lanka.

better yet maybe i should go into my brothers room and steal his books on stocks and bonds. lord knows i need to learn how a s&p 500 mutual fund works before i die. he told me that some donut company was just about to go public and i should jump in and sell high at the end of the week. (what does that mean?)

i think that was his way of saying he loved me, i think. he cared about my finances therefore he cared about me. or something. maybe. every time i tell him i'm going somewhere or want to buy something he jumps in with how much the company is worth and whether i should buy or hold their company. how a person can see people and clothing as mere products & numbers is so fascinating to me.

i should call my younger brother asa. i always felt bad because i think i should have fed into his life a lot of great wisdom. we talk in length now and then, though it is consistently very surface. not that i want it to be surface, but because i can never think of anything deep to say during the conversation. and when i want to tell him how much i care, or some coming of age lesson i have learned it usually comes out sounding like "keep your chin up tiger," or "the sun will come out tomorrow."

he must think i am a complete moron. so i might as well just shut my mouth like i do, that way i look introspective and quasi deep when in all reality i am thinking about the frozen burrito i had last night and how it compared to the taco bell burrito i had the night before that; wondering which is better nutritiously speaking.

-ring—ring

"aa-low"

"asa"

"what's up, whose this?"

"… ayden"

"oh hey, what's up?"

"nothing here, just about to head off to hang out with some friends, what are you up to?." lying through my coffee stained teeth.

"im going to the football game with all the guys and marilyn, some new girl i've been hanging out with." we both knew that he wasn't just being modest, he ran the school and that most girls enjoyed his company. he got the looks in the family, my older brother got the brains, and i got the …

"-yea, well sounds great man, is the team doing well this year?" trying to sound interested in his after school activities.

"no, this is the first game of the season, so …"

"yea, yea" i said, trying to sound somewhat knowledgeable, "i know, its just i really don't care about stupid high school football, im all about texas, you know."

"yea, i never liked baseball,"

damn, when did he get this honest? maybe he has always been this honest and i never … "how are they doing this year anyway?"

"yea, great, really good" i hoped.

"cool."

"yea cool."

"all right i'm off to the game, you should come by some time, mom talks about you 'missing out on my life', its rather funny really."

"even if i did stop by your never home"

"i know, its not a big deal, really."

"ok. well. hey asa …"

"yea?"

think, think

"the sun will come out chin tiger."

(awkward silence)

"… yea, will do ayden"

"yea"

"bye."

"all right man bye …"

-click

what was that? the sun will come out chin tiger?, what am i thinking? that's all i have to say? i haven't seen him in weeks, maybe a month and that's all i muster out, i can't even get a generic inspirational quote out!

i am pathetic.

maybe i should stop by, entertain my mom and her off hand (but honestly not meaning to be mean) comments. eat her all nutritional "casserole surprise", no saturated fat, no sugar, and absolutely tasteless dish she usually makes. she somehow got the impression it was my favorite, probably because i am the only one that doesn't complain out loud when she makes it.

i'll smile during our conversation. laugh, pretend my job satisfaction is at an all time high. tell her my big plans for the coming year at university. i have money in the bank, saving up for a house with a white picket fence, and once i have purchased it ill make sure the front door is painted red (just like better homes and gardens says to do for the neo-classic look that's so big in the new england area right now!) you know.

ill tell her that i have a girl in mind named wendi, and i am just about ask her to "go steady". tell her about the art piece i sold, pretend like it is not the same piece i talk about over and over, and act as though it was not asa who bought it.

i wonder if she knows that it was asa and keeps it a secret like her part time strip job on the side. maybe asa gave it to her for like a mothers day gift and she didn't know i did it so she put it in the closet because 'God did a better job' and thus she didn't need a photo of it. or maybe she did know it was me and still thought God did a better job the first time around.

tent knees.

NEW CHAPTER
you have no idea how hard it is to write a romantic comedy with homeless men.

9 a.m., wow i am utterly impressed. this is sleeping in for me, and one of the latest that i can recall. today i actually have plans. plans to leave early to work. i promise i will be out of this apartment by 1pm. my exquisite breakfast menu includes my older brothers leftover pizza that was out on the counter overnight, and some almost dated chocolate milk. not that i enjoy random combinations of inevitable heartburn, but that its convenient and the fact is toast takes to long.

my plans are quite tolerably as i scheme to take 2 bus's to get to the bauhaus. one across first street (which is free) and one that takes me up pike (which costs). the idea is that when i get off the first street bus, there is a waiting station for public transit quite close. there i will sit and wait. for what? for whom? i have no idea. (wait i just asked myself a question and answered it myself, just like the bookstore lady! what have i become? there i did it again.)

so back to the plan. i love to people watch. i put on neo-classical music in my headphones, bands like 'sigur ros' or 'rachels,' and watch as the people around me make the opera/theatrical performance of a lifetime come alive. some call this 'people watching'; i rather call it 'real time interpretive dance.'

i just stare off and let the characters set the stage, the mood, and whether the story is a tragedy, drama, or better yet a romantic comedy … which is yet to happen but i would love my mind to wonder in that general direction. although at first it was wonderfully acceptable, i find that homeless people were typically the stars in my real time interpretive dance, but now are a bit played out. much like bill murray in broken flowers, they just end up playing the same character in different settings.

homeless men can sit in one place for hours on end. it is incredible. they just sit, and waste so much time. its as if they are trying to speed up the slow grip of death by allowing atrophy to prematurely set in, or it may be that they just really have no where to be.

they probably have nowhere to be. you have no idea how hard it is to have a romantic comedy with homeless men in your head.

if a beautiful women dropped her scarf in slow motion the homeless guy would probably bend down and either wear the scarf himself or ask her for a dollar for returning it. sad, but i believe it to be true. i cannot stand homeless women, just the site of any women or child that is homeless makes me cringe, i want to help them i really do! i want to reach out and magically make them disappear to a realm of endless buffet's and fold out couches, a land that never rains, snows, or gets to hot or to cold. but i do not know how to begin to help, but i have tried. one fall evening i saw a homeless woman staring endlessly into her giant plastic bag, i approached her and after giving her some fast food i had ordered i asked her if i could just hug her. stunned she apprehensively said yes, i am not sure who needed it more.

all street people have monologs, real life scripts they have memorized. i hate the elaborate stories of family members who need surgeries, or the imaginary car that's parked on the other side of town that's out of gas. i love when there honest and just ask for beer money, i never give them any money but their honesty is refreshing.

my favorite scripted dialog was on summit street when a guy came up to me and said. "i've got a gun, i just need 10 cents for the bullet." i had no idea what that meant, but it made me laugh. i gave him a couple of bucks i think because of the unique story presented. street people are going to have to get creative either with their stories and signs, the competition is getting fierce. and what about technology. they need to invest into a machine where we can swipe our debit cards and type in an amount. who carries cash anymore? but i am jaded on just handing people money anymore.

once i went into a store and bought a women 2 entire grocery bags full of food. she had said that her kids were @ home and starving, and she needed at least 5 dollars to feed the three of them. i bought every staple i could think of with her by my side. orange juice, milk, bread, meat, peanut butter, and baby ruth's. after we checked out she asked for the receipt and i had no idea why. after i walked several yards away i saw the lady abruptly turn around, walk right back into the store we had just visited, and walk out empty handed. i was so confused. i approached her and asked her what happened to the groceries, and she said she knew a place across town that she could get them cheaper.

i was informed by the store owner minutes later that the women was a former methadone recipient who had drifted back into her heroin addiction. and she often swindles tourists and tenderfoots.

i cant tell you how used i had felt at that moment. every last (and i thought obsolete) piece of good that was left in me had been betrayed by this women who looked like she had just been beat up twice by the ugly stick and had not slept in days. she was supposedly out hunting for food for her ethiopian children that i had probably seen on a world hunger relief commercial; but the shocking realization that i was just a gullible idiot hit me below the belt.

what will become of her … that lady is trying today to get the high she had the first time by betraying peoples trust and discouraging the belief that mankind as a whole is innately good. she is the holocaust, she is vietnam,

she is … only human.

so here i sit, staring off into people. besides writing screen plays in my head upon unwilling thespians i love to just sit silently and peer off into the commoners imagining what they are thinking about at that very second.

i just wish i knew. if i could have any super power that would be it. i promise i wouldn't use it for evil. i just want to know that people are thinking subconsciously or consciously the same things i am. i promise.

i see all sorts of people writing in journals @ work each day. sometimes i just want to steal one or two. delve into the their heads, read their thoughts like a medium reads palms. i desire direly to read their minds, hopes, dreams, fears, & lusts.

to my shame i must admit that i hope each day that someone forgets theirs, for i will take it home and study it like a graphic novel or a text book on the in and out of the homosapien species 101. maybe make photo copies and return them to the rightful yet forgetful owner.

i count mine as sacred, even though it is shallow writings of nothingness, and they in turn hold theirs as sacred; though i am almost positive that everyone else's is most probable to be profound eye opening theories of life and all that it entails. as a result none are ever lost or forgotten here @ the coffee shop and i am left to question curiously what is in those fatigued manilla pages.

i once heard that the average human has 16 conversations with themselves in their head every minute. i think i have 16 questions per minute, not conversations, because i do not have anything quite figured out to have a complete conversation. but why do we as the human species want to know what everyone else around us are thinking? honestly i think its because i want to see if they have the same questions i do. i want to figure out if inadequacy is a norm or a subculture genre. or maybe because for once in my life i want to feel normal. i want to know if everyone around me is as crazy as i am.

or normal.

normal.
just normal.

NEW CHAPTER
an introduction to
dr. husmillo's gratitude

off to the rest of the way to work. i've been at this public transportation hub way to long. i wish there was a way i could go in get my pay check and then leave and call in sick. its not that i have something better to do today then work, but sunday morning television could hold my attention better than this job.

its so mundane, so prosaic, so jejune, so insipid, so lifeless … and the job isn't much better.

i am not going to work. its not like i can spend any of that paycheck anyway. i got all the way up to the door, and at the last second kept walking. i wonder if they saw me, i wonder if brian the shift manager saw me and is now calling a staff meeting to reinforce punctuality and avoiding responsibility when @ the door of your perspective job.

i walked home, why did i come back to my apartment? my rooms a mess, its frustrating to walk into all that mess, but even more frustrating is to work on my room for an hour, stand back and realize it looks no better. my mother was somewhat of a perfectionist, or at least i believe she found her self worth in how the cleanliness of her habitation, or how other perceived her habitation. thus now i am left with a sense of incompleteness and almost irksome when my room is left unkempt. nature vs. nurture? nurture win's this round.

cold pizza crusts and dated chocolate milk for lunch. i am seriously starving. not like the etheopian children the homeless women swore she cared for, but starving.

no ones home. my cable is turned off, failure to comply with the bills request. that means the internet is down too. i truly hate technology, not because of anything it did, but i've just realized i have grown so codependent; my social life, my erratic addiction which has stolen hours of my life looking for new and creative web sites or bands. all for not.

unclean food and forsaken dirty dishes are strewn everywhere.

-click

-beep

"ayden this is your mom, is this an answering machine, is this on? hello … uh (background, hand clinched on phone and i faintly hear 'asa i think no ones home') well, this is your mom, i need you to call home and tell me your ok. why don't you come by the house and see your mother? you spend time with asa but not your own mother? that was very nice of you to let him spend the night last night. your a good brother. call home son, or just come over, ill make us your favorite casserole dish! ok bye for now."

so my brother told her he stayed here. i better remember that in case she brings it up. i did the same thing to my older brother; asa probably went out on the town with all the boys, they drank a little to much bourbon and had a limo escort them downtown. when they finally did get to the game the quarterback got hurt on the first play. no one knew how to throw a football suddenly and they looked to the stands and a huge spotlight focused on my brother. he stood up handed his cell phone and bourbon on the rocks to the a tall brunet that was on his left, though he winked to the blond on his right as he ran towards the field.

he threw with perfect accuracy and scored 19 ½ touchdowns, got drafted by the texas tumbleweeds that very night, was the school hero, voted class president, and won the lottery all in the same night. lost track of time with the blond and brunet in their 14th story condo with a view of the entire inner coastal and said he spent the night with me, thus missed his ride to school and has woken up with an unexplainable headache. ok so he probably woke up with a headache, and i am sure he didn't explain why.

there is nothing to do in this apartment. i really should read. but the only books i own are those in which i have already read, and i hate reading books twice, really what is the point. its like a movie, you know the ending, you know the dialogue, why would you read/watch anything twice. i never got why people would watch animated tv shows and/or movies over and over again. i think they do it just so they can memorize the lines each character says and say them back and forth; then once out in a social setting repeat them with people who have nothing better to do with their lives then sit there and memorize pointless movie/tv show lines too. no original thought of their very own, and they replace conversational 'whit' with memorization techniques.

well tonight there is always my brothers classics such as '11 steps to financial freedom', 'rich dad, poor father', or the ever thrilling climatic read 'motley fools guide to your money markets."

out of the entire galaxy my whole world has collapsed to this. my apartment. i could be walking around the city, but i have already been, so im here. not in my right mind, but here. in my apartment.

i begin to wonder around my apartment as if its new, wow what is this? i wonder how long this water bong has been here, there's still old water, looks like a film has built up like algae on the top. oh god, that is the most foul smell, i think i accidentally just spilled some. crap. i wonder when the last time this ash tray has been emptied. do not worry fellow roommates, i will pitch in and help, i've got it. the ashtray is empty. well i'm done working, time for a break. i browse through the kitchen as if in the refrigerator something new will have appeared in it magically within the last 10 minutes.

"shazaam"

nope nothing new. i open up the cabinets to see our bread count. i hate wheat bread, but my brother thinks that white 'doesn't contain a lot of necessary vitamins and nutrients.' at least my mom got through to someone. upon opening the counterfeit wood cabinets i discover something that i had yet not seen.

there were 3 bottles of 2002 blackstone merlot laying on their sides precariously in the simulated cabinet. my brother doesn't drink so this shocked me to no end. but upon further investigation and examination i made a discovery. as i studied the evidence, i noticed that there was a small, open faced card taped on the side of the bottle.

'to my all time favorite broker,
thank you for your help, you are an asset to me and my family. your investment tips have been not only invaluable but notably profitable.
cheers,
-dr. husmillo'

well this is evidence we are going to have to take to the lab for further analysis.

i don't even grab a cup, what is the use, its just one more piece of garbage that will never get out of my room anyway. i never really acquired a taste for wine, its like a tart tasting knife stabbing the back of my throat, but man this stuff messes me up so fast. it hurts less and less in my throat the more and more i drink.

occasionally my mouth will pucker, but the more i drink the more that seems to stop to. it starts to feel like a warm jacuzzi sliding down my esophagus. i fiddle with some clothes trying to sort them into clean and dirty, but i end up throwing them all together, lumping into one giant pile. then i try to sort them into colors, darks, and towels. but again that is in vain because now im feeling dr. husmillo's thanksgiving gratitude pretty well. whenever i try to throw a towel into the towel pile it seems to land in the darks or fall tragically short. back to the kitchen.

"shazaam"

nope nothing in the fridge still, unless i can concoct something out of cottage cheese, 1/2 a yellowing avocado, and ketchup packets from some fast food restaurant. guess it's back to the formal introductions with my new found friend.

NEW CHAPTER
for dramatic effect in any melodramatic movie carry around a half bottle of wine.

the second bottle of wine seemed much harder to open then the first. obviously the cork must have been put in tighter for some reason. child lock maybe. well wine doesn't taste so bad, now. i think i have officially acquired a taste. my face doesn't pucker, and nothings stabbing my throat or chest that i can feel. back to my room, well this place doesn't look so bad. the sun is going down but still it is rather bright, brighter than i remember it being a couple minutes ago. and i think my room is on a tilt a whirl, and those always made me nauseous just looking at them at the city fair. ill just lay down.

ok no. as soon as i close my eyes the entire earth rotates in opposite directions and i want off this ride. i stumble to the kitchen, i must look like a clumsy tango dancer during a pubescent growth spurt with his shoes tied together.

i need to get something to eat. cottage cheese. no. ketchup packets. maybe. no. i stumble back towards my room but end up in len, our foreign roommates, room. he is so protective of his room, its all so tidy, perfectly placed together as if each item is in alphabetical order. i swear to the god's that he makes his bed every morning, maybe he sleeps on top of them because they are always so military straight looking. i mean really who does that?

im surprised that the door is not locked, or better, that there isn't a booby-trap made of carpet look-a-like substance, but really its a 12 foot hole with metal spikes protruding waiting ominously at the bottom. his room all looks so white-anglo-saxon normal, though he is foreign. complete with the random rap/hip-hop artist poster, which is something i never got. here you have all these people singing along and empathizing with these rappers who are from the inner city who have been shot at and raised in an entirely different culture. how do they, the listeners, all seem to relate with the artist? i will never fully understand.

the other poster in the room is another hot air brushed girl in strings of clothing, which they call a bikini, on some foreign beach no one will actually visit because it was designed in photoshop, with that 'please take me' look.

'xoxo britny' it says.

stated, but never meant.

the only thing that stands out as a little peculiar is the 3 foot gun safe next to his desk. its a combination, fire proof, superman proof, box. no seriously i think this is kryptonite on the handle. though i try to make up three lucky numbers even now, it never opens. but this time its going to be different.

13-7-27 why not, those sound, good.

click click 13

click-7

click click click-27.

"shazaam"

nothing.

its still locked. im still spinning, and just want to get something in my stomach besides blackstone at this point, anything to make this upside down ferris wheel ease for even just a second. i go over to the desk thinking that maybe, just maybe, there might be a health bar or a frozen dinner in his desk drawer.

nothing.

pens, receipts, blank envelopes, an empty rolling stones jewel case, and a silver revolver.

a silver revolver?

i proceed to pull it out and examine it. i've never actually held a hand gun before. i obviously voted against them because i put 'democrat' on my voters registration card, but never held one; for how small they are they sure are heavy. i tote the loaded weapon out of the room mumbling lines from various movies (which i had seen more than once) where handguns where imperative to the scene.

back in my room i grab the wine bottle because a gun in one hand and a bottle of deep red wine in the other just makes for a dramatic effect for any movies martini shot. i need music, in my cd player goes my blonde redhead cd on repeat. track number 2 on the album 'misery is a butterfly' is perfect for this take. i turn it up so loud the neighbors would complain if they were home from their cubical white collar job.

there is a mirror at the end of our shabby apartment hallway and it is there were i practice my lines for various scripts. taking a chug from my wine i wipe my hand on my sleeve and begin to waive the gun like a hand gesture.

my monologue begins, and for some reason i've abruptly acquired the accent of an italian mobster.

"so where were you last night?"

-

"is that so?"

-

"i thought you said you didn't love him"

-

"I THOUGHT YOU SAID YOU DIDN'T LOVE HIM"

-

"why? why are you doing this? i could have given you the world, but instead you took the equivalence of a 3rd world country."

ok new scene, that was no good & that last line was god-forsakingly blear-eyed. i want something a little more deadly a little more man-o-mystery stuff.

"you know i have to do this. its for us. its how i make my money, you know that."

-

"just one more job, one more job little woman, i promise."

-

"his name?" i chug some wine and wipe my mouth on my sleeve, "you want his name? his name is cash, brennan cash."

-

(ok this scene i like because maybe she is in love with cash or it's like her brother or something. or father. yes her father, who used to beat her. and she is all for it.

no. the hit man wouldn't make any money knocking off an abusive father, so brennan cash has to be her lover—who is coincidentally another hit man.)

"why, why wont you let me kill him?"

-

"you what?"

-

"but for how long, my god how long have you loved him?"

-

then decide him or me!"

(the barrel of the gun was purposefully raised to my furrowed brow to show her that i was serious. and i began to shout at my imaginary confused lover with her long brown her and browned italian skin, all with wine in one hand spilling on the floor of our 5 star hotel carpet floor. the drapes were closed for secrecy and i was in a pinstriped suit with my shirt open and my tie hanging loose. my catholic joan of arc medallion is swinging frantically in rhythm with every sway of my arms. oh this is good.)

"THEN DECIDE HIM OR ME!!!"
-

but as the silver revolver rested on my temple the song fittingly ended in my room. the scene ended in silence and i had just spilled wine on our apartment hallway carpet. but that wasn't my concern.

my concern was the sudden catharsis of how comfortable this gun felt resting upon my ashen temple.

NEW CHAPTER
the unwilling clarity

i walked to my room and the music began to repeat the same song distractingly loud. i unplugged the player before it could begin the songs next stanza. it's as if for a moment i had unwilling clarity. the wine lost its effect. my breathing slowed. i never took the gun from my head. it kind of rested there like it was a security blanket, as if this was some how normal for me to have a loaded revolver pointed at my own piddling brain.

it felt as if the i could see the world in tunnel vision when my hand was on the trigger. i finally surmised the entire meaning of life in 3 seconds.

1. one thousand

2. two one thousand

3. three one thousand … nothing.

there was nothing here for me. if i could be anywhere in the world i would want to be asleep. i want to have that content look on my face, i do not care if it is stapled there. at least i will know that it is going to be there.

reflecting on my life there wasn't much to it. no love to speak of. no laughter noteworthy. no accomplishment that deserves a statue, or plaque of any sort. no friendships that will be missed. no family reunions that will miss my company. my job will hire someone new, my photographs will be lost in the attic and eventually tossed away, or used to wrap the precious china with when eventually someone moves. what ever is beyond this is better than what is behind me. i don't want to write a note because i do not want to set down the wine or the gun. i should do it now so they can find me before i smell up the apartment and they lose their security deposit due to an unknown foul smell in the guest bedroom.

i always wondered what the last thought of a person who knows they are going to die would be. and mine was about security deposits.

now i am sure i am pathetically commiserable.

all's well that ends …

i chug the wine, i rationalized that if it eventually numbed the stabbing in the back of my throat that it could help with any pain i was about to feel. i wiped my mouth with my sleeve …

for dramatic effect.

-click
-click
wait wait not my head i want a look of content on …

'BLAMMMMKKKKKKSSSS'
'BLAMMMMKKKKKKSSSS'

PROLOGUE
... is this heaven,
or is there silence in hell too.

awake. no one is in here.

hello ...

i try to talk but nothing comes out.

claustrophobic. the lights are off. the room is dark. it feels like time has stopped. am i dead? is this all there is (-bblep). am i just conscience breathing outside my body even though im dead. i cant be dead. oh God, please no. God im sorry. really. please don't tell me that i will have my eyes open at the funeral, but my face will look like im asleep. then they will put me in the ground.

claustrophobia.

oh this cant be it. quietude. silence. (clre-bbleeep) im awake. someone help. lull. i didn't want to to die. not like this not this. not ever. God please. i don't want to die like this.

.... ohh my f-ing head
where am i?
oh god, my insides are burning.
cant see strrraaiiggh.... think thin ...

days, maybe.
"ayden?"
"God?"
"no."
"i dontt know wwhheerre i, i...."

-
-fuzz

68

"i don't know what to tell you mam"

"what can we do now?"—fuzz

"wait, pray, or both, right now we can not tell the extent of damage internally."

-fuzz

-

"ayden, can you see me?"

hush.

"whose there, i cant see anything."

"i have to go wake her up, don't go back to sleep"

"i cant help it. just so tired."

"don't you dare ayden, you owe it to her!"

thoughts seem to piece themselves together so slowly, as if my mind is trying to put together a jigsaw pieces from three different puzzles. my whole body aches, but why. i can hear and feel every beat of my heart, my whole body is pulsating in my ears. something is crushing every rib in my chest, it feels like someone is literally sitting on my chest. get them off, whoever it is its really not funny anymore. though i can only squint it looks as though something's penetrating the vein of my right hand and its attached to a clear tube filled with liquid. i would trace it to where they lead but it feels like my head would roll off if i move it to far one way or the other. i feel in a haze, half awake, half in an uncomfortable amount of pain. my eyes are open now. i think im in a white room. did i get into a horrible car accident, what am i doing here?

but then in a flash of panic, furry, and emergency it all comes back to me in a jolt when

"AYDEN, how could you, oh god ayden, how could you! oh thank God your alive"

"i'm ..."

"you had us all so scared, and why, honestly what reason could you have, what could have been that terrible that you could have done this to yourself!"

"i'm"

"your what! ayden, i've been here day and night wondering if i was going to ever hear from my son, again." my mother says all of this seemingly without taking in any oxygen and all with a face full of red anger slowly melting back to white, but replaced by hordes of tears.

"i'm tired mom."

"ayden, im sorry, i shouldn't have yelled, oh please don't shut your eyes. ayden, i don't want to lose you. oh God, please don't let him die. not now. please ayden don't go to slllleeee..... ."

-fuzz

-

awake. no ones in here.

hello ... i try to talk but nothing comes out. the lights are off. the room is dark. it feels like time has stopped. was that it? am i dead? is this all there is? am i just conscience with my body even though i am dead.

i once heard about this lady who underwent anesthesia before an operation and woke up half way through. she could feel them digging in her body, and see what they were pulling out, but her mouth couldn't move and try as she might she couldn't wake up. besides being locked in a small enclosure that was slowly filling up with water, waking up during a surgery would be my 2nd biggest fear. and now i think my fear is realized, but surprisingly i am placid. maybe this is what death feels like, a short fade to black and some exit music. this means i will have my eyes open at the funeral, but my face will look like i am asleep. then they will put me in the ground.

suddenly my hands start to sweat in fear, or at least i think they are sweating.

someone listen. im awake.

someone help. i don't want to to die. not like this not this, not ever. but as i struggle to open my eyes, i see that i'm in the dim lit hospital room. my mother is collapsed over the guest chair. it must be early morning, i hear the shuffling of footsteps outside my door, voices, lots of voices.

i want to wake her up, and tell her that i am sorry, but i do not, because, well i'm ashamed. this is the worst part of it so far, having to look at my mother.

"mother." my voice husky, low, torn. "mother mom."

"... ayden? ayden, oh sweetheart," her voice also husky, low, and torn.

"mom, i'm sorry, i really don't know what happened."

"you don't have to talk about it now, rest. i am just glad that your conscience, we can talk when you've rested up."

"thanks mom, thank you for staying."

this was the first time in my life i have ever had to see my own failure reflected in someone else's face. nothing in life has ever felt worse.

"ayden, i love you, regardless of what you did, or have done, or will do in the future, just know i love you," she said with such urgency, as if she were rehearsing her speech for any few seconds she might have left with me.

and for that moment i felt it. sure we say i love you in our family, but its so nonchalant.

so meaningless.

so ... stated.

she was my mother, i was her son. floods of memories came back. me age 6. i had just broke my mothers german antique clock, it was a family heirloom. one of the only possessions her family brought over on the boat from germany. she looked at it and then looked at me, and with tears in her eyes said.

"ayden, this clock meant the world to me, but it was just a clock, you are my son, and no matter what you do i will love you."

sure i got beat around a little by my dad & grounded for life without parole for breaking it, but those words never left my head. i meant more than things that meant the most.

i am in trouble. i don't know how but i know i am in trouble. i have psychological analysis's, surgeries, and consequences to face. life is going to change, whether i fight, or i concede, its going to change.

NEW CHAPTER
there is a serene lullaby
in chaos & ataxia.

add 2 months later to the story.

so they have determined that i am not 'insane', but diagnosed bipolar ii, meaning there is constant presence of more than one episodes of abnormally elevated moods, 'mania' as it is reffered to clinically. my next six months are planned out for me, like a rerun of the dogmatic's of high school. three months are here in a low security voluntary hospital 'help' ward where my entire life is supervised, then three months in a psychological 'half way house,' where i will be allowed to see family, and friends. none of it is really mandatory by government standards, but i think it eases the conscience of the doctor's, but more importantly my mother.

they figure if i voluntarily go through all this crap than i am probably serious about not attempting it again. its kind of come and go as you please in the ward, though as i learned right away its almost too serene to leave.

sometimes there is peace in chaos. a serene lullaby in disorder and the anarchy of life. one just has to listen.

so far i have yet to see anyone overtly "demented" like you do on the movies. no one here thinks they are 'elvis presley' or 'Jesus Christ.' most people here are depressed and admit it, or are depressed and don't. there are some who space out frequently, a lot of older people. a couple schizophrenics that look (and smell) more like street people than mentally unstable.

i've had a lot of time to replay the events of the last couple months over and over, coming to terms with what exactly i did, but still not sure who i am.

i shot myself, twice. the second shot was more reflex and not so much commitment to kill myself. in retrospect i never thought that i would actually go through with it. it just … happened.

the first bullet passed right under my heart, and i would have been dead if my roommate would not have showed up shortly there after and the paramedic stopped the loss of blood. the second bullet simply careened the surface skin, caressing my rib cage with clemency. there are several complications, some which could be fatal over time, but the doctors will not know for some time. more tedious tests but i should know my fate, or lack there of shortly.

i was there, in the heat of the moment. death, she wooed, i gave in. she loved me when no one else would. i honestly tried to kill myself, and failed.

i have surrendered to change. i need to move on in my life. i am not looking for success, i am looking for normality. i do not want to be superman, i just want to be human. i do not expect to obtain, just overcome. i do not want a life, i just want to live.

i've only been here a short while but i have already memorized this entire place; every wall, every chair, every magazine, and book. i never really talk to anyone, i rationalized that if i keep to myself then it will force me to 'come to grips with my emotions' as they so eloquently put it, and get me out of her in a timely manner. i once proceeded to count the number of tiles on the ceilings but after a short while i stopped, questioning only then my sanity.

looking around the room i see that these people all seem to be keeping to themselves. and it makes me wonder if that is why they ended up here in the first place. can loneliness drive someone to need therapy?

think about it: if everyone you knew left you, abandon you, or passed away and you had to recluse to your own demise in solitude, in the same house for years upon years, dementia seems like the natural evolution of the human psyche.

then you have the never-ending time-enduring question of "what is normal." maybe these people really live in this alternate universe, who are we to tell them that what we know to be reality really is?

listen to me, i keep saying things like 'they' and 'them' as if i am not in the same four walls as these people. "they" were sane enough not to have a high noon, ok corral gun fight with themselves.

two old men look out the opposing window, they are not so much talking as communicating in mumbles. there is an elderly women murmuring something to herself. actually i am not sure if she is a man or a women, but (they) wear a dress. the only time she talks in more than just a whisper is when anyone of the asian persuasion walks past. that is when she seems to lift herself out of her wheelchair, like a pushup, and shout 'gerrymander!! gerrymander!' i intend to ask her what the significance in such an act actually means, in time.

realizing that everyone in the room, including myself, are all sitting down or are in wheel chairs, except for one person. from the back i could see that the shirt probably didn't originally belong to them, and her hair looked like it had been bleached, but not in the last month or two. when she finally did turn around she looked straight at me and i felt caught like i had been staring at her back for some time.

oh how i hate that, you know when your looking at someone because they look different or they are just gorgeous and on your fourth glance up ohhh they catch your eyes in the dead of a day dream glare. which i was. she started a steady and sudden march in my direction like the trip over was a fourth of july parade. she looked like she didn't belong in here. i thought all near attractive girls had it all figured out. the closer she came the more extraordinary she looked.

"im a nurse here," she said, almost demanding.

"you don't look like a nurse."

"its my day off"

"why did you come to work on your day off"

"i like the food here"

"the food here taste like … well hospital food."

"yea, well its free."

at this point it felt like she should light up a lucky stike, well that's what happens in the independent movies.

"why don't you go into the cafeteria to eat with all the other nurses?"

"you crazies make me feel normal."

"that's kind of harsh don't you think?"

"harsh but true. honestly i don't feel like i have to be normal here. so i ask the other nurses to treat me like a patient."

"sounds, well … like your lying."

"well, believe what you want."

"what's your name?"

"whose asking?"

"well, i just, (saying 'i asked you first' seemed quite elementary at this point) my name is ayden."

"its nice to meet you, my name is nico."

and with that she walked away, pretended to talk to another patient, held their wrist like she was taking his pulse, and then just walked away before there was even a remote chance she could tell what their pulse really was. i don't think the old man even knew she was there. she walked down the patient room hall and out of sight.

NEW CHAPTER
withered hands tell endless parables
if only you take the time to listen

usually i can fall asleep right away in this place but tonight i cant seem to keep my eyes closed. typically the meds put me to sleep, well that plus the fact that really i have nothing in life to worry about.

when the majority of you life is spent wallowing in the gravel, and you sink even lower than that in one night with two bullets, its only up from here. but tonight, tonight i cant sleep. i keep replaying my conversation with nico, she has been the only thing not jejune about time here. wondering if she really was a nurse. i haven't seen her for two days now. maybe she was a part-time nurse.

"sir, have you seen nico today?" i asked the asian 'gerrymander' nurse assisting me with my meds.

"i don't know if we have a nico here."

"well she was here two days ago, but i haven't seen her since, i think she is just a part-time."

"part time what?"

"nurse."

"nope, there is no nurse here named nico that i know of."

"is there a patient named nico on this floor."

"i can check, maybe we admitted a patient on the floor in the last couple of days and i have yet to learn their name."

moments later the nurse came back over to me and put his hand on my shoulder, as if he was about to tell me a family member had died or something.

"i'm so sorry ayden, but there is no patient by that name either."

maybe he thought i was delusional. but with vainglorious lips and glassy emerald eyes like hers she could be anything she wanted.

now it haunted me. not that i was suddenly entranced by this girl, but that she was a perplexity. and to be honest i don't have a lot on my mind, except not wanting to miss taco tuesdays here in the ward cafeteria or morning group (because they serve orange juice and those donut holes.) ok so i am entranced by this girl. she haunts me like none other, and i don't even know if she is a patient here anymore.

its not that i am falling in love by any means i am not even sure what love 'feels' like. its that i am falling for the mystery of something i cannot grasp, someone i can not yet figure out and psychoanalyze in my own way.

i adopted a grandmother while living here in this hospital. i am no psychologist, but i think the only reason she is here is because no one else wanted her. she is precious, her wrinkles tell endless parables, her orphaned crystal blue eyes tell even more narratives. she smiles even though the rest of her face reads of despair, i am sorry that was such a bad analogy but that was the only way i can explain it.

her name was billy, and on more than one occasion she showed me the pictures of her when she was young and beautiful, full of life and insouciant smiles. she told me all about her life; her marriage to her seaman husband who had fought in world war two and later of her 2 children. the stories were fascinating, and it was as if a book had suddenly come alive, i hung on every word and lesson.

i will never forget the day when she taught me my biggest lesson, the end of mortality. she stated somberly that her son only visited her once a year and she had yet to see her grandchild. billy told me each morning she wondered if she was going to die that day, and if not then, then when?

"isn't that why i am in here? i cannot leave, i have no freedom, no car, no self administered decision, and i am in here ... seemingly just waiting to die."

the game room/cafeteria suddenly fell quiet for me when she said that. the patterned wrinkles on her face were soon covered with wordless tears and my heart lay upon the floor where she so subtly carved it with those whetted few words. no one cared, no one remembered her name, the accomplishments were gone, the awards decayed, her dreams forgotten, the love of her life, dead. her son didn't care. her friends, gone. oh how selfish i am, for within her tears i thought not of the heart ache of this elderly women, but of my own failure to make a lasting impact on someone else's life.

i am her son. she was here and i never visited her. i never tell my own mother how much she matters to me. this women, billy, is my own mother years down the road. what impact have i made on anyone's life? especially on those i consider the closest. my own blood. i have been so self entwined and self absorbed with my own shortcomings and problem's that i have failed to see that there are hundreds of thousands of men and women in my own city with real problems, real hurts, real hell.

i feel so fake.

i am plastic,

a pseudo anything.

i feel so dead.

tears now stream down my egoistic face not for her but for the fact that i am so surface.

so superficial.

narcissistic.

i confessed this all to billy. i repented for how depth-less i was. thanked her over and over for what she had shown me. honestly her melting eyes were better than any therapy this place could ever give. she then quoted me something i will never forget for the rest of my existence. she said that this catharsis for me reminded her of a muslim man by the name of rumi once said:

"when you are dead, seek for your resting place

not on the earth, but in the hearts of men."

she was happy she had rested in my heart, for me billy left me with a sense of urgency to love while i still can, create while my hands are not yet frail, give of myself while my heart is not yet full, think while my ideas are still my own, run away while freedom is still an option and set my course so that one day I may remain in the hearts of men, forever.

billy died within 4 weeks of meeting her. tears never fell for billy, not that i wasn't sad, but for me she was like plato. she had lived long enough to instill her philosophy in me, her student, then become a martyr. eternally in the heart of a man forever.

i was furious that i never saw her son even after she died he did not as much come to collect her belongings they just sat there for weeks. i wanted to beat his face in, i wanted to tell him that she died with the thoughts of her unseen grand-son holding her mind captive. i do not think it was age that killed billy, it was the freedom from heartache in death she sought. i kept the pictures she showed me, i did not want the memories of a better time to be thrown away never to be seen or cared about again.

"hi" nico said with a half smile, as if she were plotting something. not now. i wanted to say. but it came out sounding like,

"and where have you been the last, little while."

"why have you missed me?"

"no, no, not at all, its just that trying to hold a conversation with gerryman-der-lady is quite hard unless you have a stethoscope or your asain."

she laughs, and it kind of catches me off-guard.(i think back on all the times i have made girls laugh and i cant remember one time that a girl laughed at my whit and not at my self inflicted humiliation).

"are you always so funny?"

"actually no, my family never got the humor gene, but we did get the dna pre-disposition for back hair."

"you are funny." as again she laughs out loud, and i again am caught off guard.

"no really."

silence. then.

"so why did you do it ayden?" she said as she was lost in a gaze out the window just behind me.

"do what?"

"shoot yourself. why did you shoot yourself."

"wow, are you always so blunt this seasonably in a friendship?" i said thinking that i never thought the honesty extended in small group time would come back to haunt me in such a precarious way.

"do you always cower from honesty this early in your life ayden?"

"why would you think i dodge honesty?"

"because those most afraid of honesty are either not honest or most afraid."

"so why aren't you honest nico?"

"what do you mean?"

"well you said you were a nurse."

"your trying to get off the subject, we were talking about why you shot your-self."

at first her honesty was refreshing, now it was making me unusually irritated.

"tell me why you lied to me and told me you were a nurse."

"well, i think there is a huge line between lying and extending your imagina-tion. i was mealy extending my imagination."

"this is getting rather juvenile. that's called lying; hence the opposite of truth."

"ayden, when i make up a new profession or 'character' in my head it relieves the tension that i am facing, understanding that my charades are a temporal solu-tion for temporal problems. but it appears you think trying to kill yourself would relieve your tension, a permeant solution to temporary problems. so now tell me, what was coursing through your head?"

"no, i honestly don't know what i was thinking, i had had a little to much to drink."

"do you think that drinking results in bad decisions, because that sounds like an excuse to me, if drinking always ended in a suicide attempt i believe the fda would begin a neo-prohibition."

"maybe."

"so really why?"

"honestly?"

"honestly."

"life, it just seems endless, endlessly overwhelming. endlessly crushing. there was really nothing left, i had done it all, i had seen it all, and at the end of the day just wasn't worth sticking around."

"you make your existence sound like like such a morbid afterthought, and i have to interject on your commentary of life and disagree. it sounds to me like you haven't experienced everything ..."

"yea, well not all, but enough."

"how can you say that, have you ever been to diminutive towns like st. joe, michigan? there is the most beautiful pier there."

"no"

"what about oahu, hawaii, or picaso's blue man and guitar?"

"well i've seen, well, no."

"what about love?"

-silence

"then you haven't seen all there is to see, you haven't experienced all there is to experience, you know nothing of this life."

"how can you say that you don't even know me."

"your face seems to tell of more anecdotes than most novels, and because without ever finding something as simple as love i argue that you have yet to have really had a life in full."

"simple? you think love is, well its irrelevant. i can honestly say that i don't know what love looks, or even feels like. love never showed me anything except a postcard from 'beautiful denver, colorado'."

"then you have never experienced a sleepless night?"

"oh i've had my fair share of those."

"no your not catching the point of a sleepless night. where yours may have been spent in fear, a person in love's night is spent in hope, in dreams, or in the secret ambition of a future."

"then why, wise sage, why haven't i ever had this romeo and juliet relationship you so articulately speak of."

"do you realize that romeo and juliet both died? they did so with the last glimpse being that of their lover, and the last thought of not wanting to live for anything else but love."

"well i never wanted to live for anything but love but all i found were the inveigle open arms of death."

"but you were never truly living. from the way you talk you probably never sought love."

"but i thought love was supposed to come to you."

"where do you read that stuff? as if this trite word 'love' has a holy text and only works in one way. the way love is conjured is not by concentrating on living life to find love but by simply living and loving life itself. it seems to strike when one stops trying to find mrs. right and start becoming mr. right."

"i don't understand this mr. right nonsense, sounds like some cosmo survey-formula."

"its not like that at all, actually i think its almost the opposite. its just most people, girls especially, try to wear all the right clothes, find all the right makeup, wear their hair just a certain way, buy certain products, and talk their certain lingo just to attract the opposite sex.

"that is not how it should be at all. people should learn a new language, learn how to paint, go travel the world over, grow plants, experience life, et cetra. and when life has had its share of you and you have taken life by the handles, love strolls in so casual. so classy. so purposefully."

"then explain my parents, within just a handful of years there marriage crumbled. they made each other so happy, but then it was over as 'purposefully' and as quickly as it began."

"that's just it, couples are continuously pursuing clumsily into committed relationships thinking that the other person is going to make them happy. when they realize that their partner cannot make them happy they end it. you have to be satisfied with yourself, and have the ability to find happiness on your own life before you can go and share your life with someone else."

"i can't and don't want to try to comprehend that; i was under the impression that love makes you happy."

"it does, but don't confuse lust with love. love can make you happy temporarily, but when your talking about happiness for an entire lifetime its different, that's commitment. imagine two blind people who have lost their way and eventually run into each other on the street. at first they are both ecstatic and elated to have found someone in a similar predicament, blind and lost. but the merriment soon wears off because even though they are together they are still lost, and blind.

eventually they will realize they are in the same quagmire as they began, only together. and that's why the majority of relationships end so wanting and desolate, they are blind and don't realize they have to be completely happy with themselves before they find someone else to live life with."

"for a little women it sounds like you have had some amazingly uncomplicated relationships in your life."

"no, i just have sought life, not the attention of the mere boys, and found answers along the way. but the greatest teacher in life is not the immediate gratification of success, but through the hindsight of failure. life is an unfair and cruel professor, it punishes you first and then gives you the lesson."

"so your not a nurse." i said with a slur & smirk.

"nope, im the ward psychologist."

"apparently."

she gets up and walk's away, and i want to ask her to go out for coffee, or something. then i realize that we are both captivates of our surroundings and just let her stroll off, hands in my face with thoughts buried in the memory of billy, envelopes postmarked denver, and a new outlook on ardency.

NEW CHAPTER
i think therefore i am ... thinking.
or at least that's what i thought.

its sad to realize that their are some prodigious and amazing childhood memories that people lose in their lifetime. i wonder if our brain work's like a computer, we have a hard drive and can only remember so much; and when your mind gets full (at probably the age of 17 or so) your mind has to start getting rid of some of the old memories to make room for the new. it starts with the meaningless quarrels with your parents about having to go to bed, than advances to christmas presents but has the uncanny ability to remember the humiliating and embarrassing moments that you try so hard to forget.

i mean, i made some heart-stirring memories with my brother's that i would love to do anything in this world not to forget!

for instance the fact is young boys are the most impressionable humans alive and will imulate anyone or anything we come in contact with, or see on television. once i recall the olympics on tv one fevered summer. so, when i was about 10, we deliberated that we were going to have our own olympics around the neighborhood. we got string from my mothers sewing kit as a finish line to our track and field event. we got in our neighbors pool and timed each other as to how long we could hold our breath, while trying to collect as many colored rings as we possibly could (i think all boys have a knack for making up games). we even had a bottle rocket distance contest from our backyard over our roof. though my brother didn't win the competition he did however succeed in making it right into the neighbors trash can and catching it on fire.

sure we got in some precarious predicaments but as kids that was one of the greatest shots with a bottle rocket we had ever seen, i remember talking about that one event for months afterward. an immediate neighborhood folklore.

but now, unless i see a firework stand on the side of the road or a random trash can on fire that memory is filed away. i would hate for small moments like that to be replaced by something i saw online, or a useless encounter with a high school friend, or where i put my keys. i hope in heaven that their is a giant database so we can sit up there and watch our entire lives over again. sure, if Jesus or your mother is sitting next to you you might want to keep the 'skip to the next chapter' remote button handy.

"time for meds ayden," my new found asian nurse friend said. i want to ask his name honestly i do, but you know when you have known someone for an extended period of time and you don't know their name its just awkward to inquire. so it goes better off unasked. i have figured out the way to solve this dilemma, you get one of your friends to come with you and you introduce your friend to the nameless person, therefore introducing two people and getting the name of the unidentified person you have known for an extended period of time.

problem: the only people in my immediate area are drooling. i am afraid its just going to have to remain awkward.

"what time is it?" i asked.

"9 am."

"well, i should have discovered these meds years ago!"

"well there not exactly over the counter." he laughed, but i didn't.

"did you ever find your friend nico?"

then it hit me, maybe he thinks i am crazy, really. here i am ranting about some fictitious nurse, knowing full well she is a delusional psychologist ... or not. describing someone he has not seen. maybe this is a test or something.

"no, i found out she is mealy a patient who is perpetual liar, she must be some kind of mental or something." i said, trying to sound as sane as possible.

"i see." he said while looking at me with this peculiar 'do you know where you are?' look.

"ayden, dr. richardson and i feel you have been very quiet in group, if you ever want to share please feel free. i think that if you listen you could learn allot from the others, and maybe they could learn a thing or two from you. that is, if you wish to contribute."

"honestly doc, what could i learn from the others in our group? i don't even think were dealing with remotely the same problems."

"i can see why you would presume that, but in essence everyone in here is dealing with very similar problems, its just the brain seems to deal with them in different ways."

"i don't believe it, i mean how is my previous disdain for life anywhere remotely close to the two guys that sit and stare out the window muttering maniacally to each other about what street they are on now, and what the good places to eat and dance in town are? one would think that those two are having the time of their lives in here!?"

"i think that you can learn something new from everyone in this room and conceivably everyone in this world. but as for those two you must realize that they are mentally betrayed into better times. they are trying to continually live out a different perception of life, one that has expelled all pain from the present. take a moment and see the world from how they do. they may be sitting there in their wheelchairs but in their mind they are wandering those streets that they stare at, laughing, running, retelling stories time and time again. realize that the mind is an amazing creation. where as some people stay inside of it, others use it to explore their surroundings."

"but that world isn't real. its an illusion."

"not to them, this is the way that they deal with pain. you dealt with it with an attempt on your life, they deal with it in false memories. there mind has weakened over the years, but their memories have not yet to dissipate."

"so what could i learn."

"that life is what you make of it. if you think it is over it is over. if you think its made of laughter and running and stories, than it is. your attitude and perception of life is what you think it to be. we once had a women named thelma in here who passed away about a year ago. her grandchildren told us that for as long as they could remember that she confessed that said she would die 'poor, insane, and without one friend.' guess how she died?"

"poor, insane, and without one friend."

"exactly, she was such a bitter old women whom no one wanted to be around. her kids split no inheritance because they had spent it all on her trying to help relieve her ineffective and exhaustive treatment. at her funeral two people showed up, only one of her son's and a pastor hired by her son. everything she said with her mouth she became. it seems you are what you think you are. you become who you require yourself to presume. and just because those two look like they are in a wheel chair does not mean they are not living out some of the best times of their entire lives 'in here'."

"back here in the real world it feels like its easier for me to allow my circumstances to dictate my life."

"i've come to realize that if we dictate our thoughts we can ordain and direct our lives. there was once a philosopher named descartes who said 'i think therefore i am' he was speaking of existence but i believe he could have expounded on his idea and said 'what i think therefore i am,' because it is not what we are but what we believe we are that molds us into reality."

i can't say that i hate my life in here. sure its monotonous, but at least i no longer hate life, im just floating along. it seems i have learned more and more about myself in such a short time. the consistency of my life is lulling and reassuring; it reminds me of my favorite aspect of high school, you always knew what tomorrow held. and the next year, and year after that. consistency. i also like that my room is not cluttered, i can think straight with minimal living. note to self. minimally live.

wow, i thought the word 'live' which implies living ... alive. maybe i want to do this. it feels like this place is giving me a second chance. like new years eve, like a passing grade, like grace.

they have let me wander outside now, i no longer have the full surveillance upon me constantly. the outdoors are like a whole new experience also. i didn't realize it but i missed the wind. it appears i've missed the point of love, and the subtle breeze makes me wonder if i have missed out on God to.

i seldom get phone calls and even if i did get a phone call the staff would prohibit me from talking. at first i thought it was because they thought i would use the phone cord to hang myself or something, but they quickly explained that it was a detox from the outside world. i think 'doc' saw through me rather quickly and soon wanted me to talk to my estranged family. i only have a short time in here left. i wonder at the most precarious moments as to what life outside will be like. i feel so at ease in here.

summer camps, or church camps for that matter, when you leave you think your totally different, all those positive messages, and pep talks. you leave and think you can change the entire universe for good, then you start slowly seeping back into the past. and by the time school rolls around, you haven't changed. in fact, all the promises you made were simply to impress that red head in the other group. i don't want this place to end like that. i do not want to live like i did, if i don't change i don't know if i would be alive to experience this place again. If i don't change for myself i need to @ least for billy, and my mom.

mentioning parents, my dad called again. what does he want? he hasn't been around for the good or bad times. now that i tried to end myself he calls? is he going to yell at me? because i wouldn't even take the time to listen, maybe ill tune him out like I did in my parents divorce court, or those lectures he would give us before he spanked us as kids. or is he going to try and give me some high intensity 'you can do it' tony robbins sermons. in which i would proceed to tell him that he wasn't there, he has no idea what my life was like, and why should i matter i obviously haven't mattered for years now, what makes this situation any different. its a lose-lose situation for him. stop calling.

"ayden, the nurse says you wont take any calls from the your family, is that true?"

"doc, its my dad. he really isn't apart of my family, if you know what i mean."

"its your call, but honestly you should give him a chance."

"why, you have no idea what that jackass has done to our home."

"ayden, do you think that since being in here that you have changed for the better in any sort of way?"

"yea, sorta."

"well than you agree that you have changed, in less than three months i see a huge change in even the way you carry yourself through these halls. how many years has it been since you have seen your dad"

"i don't know at least 5." (trying to sound like i didn't care but knowing full well its been 8 years, and a couple months.)

"so you can say you have changed in 3 months but you cant give your dad a chance to change in 5 years? i think you owe it to him, to prove to yourself that people can choose to change. but its your call."

"there is no way doc, i think i owe it to myself not to."

"well he said he was calling back tomorrow @ 11 tomorrow morning. you can tell me then."

"i can tell you now doc, no way."

"well talk tomorrow, but think about what i said."

lying in bed tonight is hard. thoughts sore from various echoes of recent conversations. but what echoes the most is not words at all, but the veracity of someone in whom attacks my life in an absolutely stimulating way. i wonder what in her life has forced her to love life, and if she loves life so much why is she in here? she is probably a news reporter for the local times doing an expose' on the inner workings of a mental hospital. she is exposing cruelty to elderly patients, or more horrid; how boring group therapy really is. or she is the ghost of someone who died in here hundreds of years ago, and has come back to warn me against a life without hope. well if she is a ghost, i hope she haunts me if even in just my dreams this evening.

and what about my dad, do i really think that he or i have changed? just because i do not hate life vehemently does that make me philosophically obligated to talk to my father.

father.

there is a word i haven't thought about in years. i'm going to do it. i am going to get on the phone and the first thing i'm going to do is cuss him out, then spit on his name, blame my attempt on him (just to make him feel like crap) then inform him that actually pol pot, stalin, and hitler were all his fault too. as soon as i hear his voice he will know to the full extent of my hatred. actually i am going to start my conversation with just that.

'hey. i despise you. stalin. see you in hell. hitler. goodbye. bay of pigs.'

NEW CHAPTER
the inconvenient convenience of reconciliation

"hello?"

"hello son, its been awhile."

"you think?."

"how's your mother."

"well, thanks."

"and your brothers, are they doing all right, staying out of trouble."

"they more or less start the trouble, but there good."

"that's great to hear. what have you been doing lately?"

"dad you don't need to dance around the circumstances, i am in a freaking mental hospital. small talk at this point seems absolutely frivolous."

"i know son, but to jump right in without knowing how you've been these last couple of years seems pretty inconsiderate."

"couple of years dad? couple? try almost 10! and your talking about this conversation being inconsiderate?"

"i tried!, honestly i did son."

"damnit, don't call me son. you haven't been my father for years. don't think you have the right to waltz into my life and call me son all of a sudden!"

"your right ayden, im sorry. its just your mother said that none of you really cared to talk or even see me, i just figured it would make your life easier if i wasn't in the picture."

"well it didn't."

"i am sorry, i'm sorry for all that has gone on in your life. your all i've thought about the last couple months. so sorry ayden."

"im fine."

"are you really? because from where i sit it doesn't look fine."

"well from where i sit allot of how you got to denver doesn't look that 'fine' either."

"i don't want to be here ayden. i've always wanted to be there."

"you have to be kidding me, who are you? you left us, YOU LEFT US! the only time you that you came back to visit us was on your business trips! you essentially fit us in to your schedule."

"son, there were no business meetings."

"what?"

"son. there is so much you never wanted to hear."

"what are you talking about?"

"now is not the time."

"what are you talking about, and now is not the time! what … do you want to wait another 10 years before we talk again? maybe that will be a good time, maybe you could take all of us to a father/son baseball game and talk of the good old days. oh wait you weren't around for all those 'good old days'."

"ayden, that is unfair … i."

"unfair? UNFAIR? you have the audacity to talk to me about what's unfair. do you even know what i look like now, did you ever go to one of my art shows, have you ever seen asa play any sport, do even know what any of us do for a living? you have made this unfair, you have started out all our lives unfair, just because of a bloody choir director!"

at that moment it's as if the world sat still, the moment of silence seemed like eternity.

-

and then is if the ability to humble had a voice i heard,

"there was no choir director …"

"what?"

"there was no choir director."

"i don't understand."

"son there is so much to tell you, i don't know what you need to know now, or even what i should tell you. especially where you are right now."

"i need to know everything, and everything now."

"do you love your mother?"

"yes, she was there, for everything."

"so did i, with everything i had."

"then why did you cheat on her dad, if she meant that much to you, why did you cheat?"

"i didn't cheat on her. she cheated on me."

"what?"

"son, it was either me or her that had to leave. in my naivety and stupidity i thought it best if i left you with her. she was an amazing mother, she loved you exceedingly more than i ever thought i could. i could never have raised you the way she did. so we came up with a plan for me to leave. i never wanted to hurt you, but it hurt so bad to even be around her that i had to disppear."

"but what about the plane tickets for 2, the choir director."

"never happened, i did move to denver. and i did remarry, but it was three years later, and to an amazing women that i met here at a church i was visiting."

"but i don't understand, why?"

"because inside i still loved your mother, deep down i knew if i fought for you and took you away from her i would take the only thing in life that meant anything to her. i couldn't do that to you, and i couldn't do that to her. i wanted to scream out the truth every time i saw you, but then i would look at her and know it would be years before a word was uttered."

"when were you going to tell us?"

"when you got married."

"why then."

"because then you would know by experience what it felt like to be so intoxicated by someone else that you would do anything to make them happy, even if it means losing time with your children. i regret my decision now, but know that who all three have become is due to the unconditional love your mother has given you."

"i … i don't know what to say. what about the choir director?"

"do you remember the choir director?"

"… no, we were all so young then, and never really thought about it."

"it was a story your mother concocted, the choir director was in her late sixties, she was moving to another city around the same time. it just seemed to be an easy escape for her story."

"but why, why couldn't you have just moved and told us you were tired of her nagging or something."

"because deep down i was trying to send your mother a message that i still would take her back no matter what, i was switching rolls with her, showing her what it would have done to her vicariously. and that is why i sent the divorce papers on valentines day. february 14 was one year to the day that i found out about your mothers affair. you see for the first year i was trying everything to try to amend our relationship, but when i called, or wrote she would never even respond. she never wanted to work it out. when i realized it was truly over two years later i happen to run into christina-marie and we began our relationship."

"i … i still don't know what to say."

"i apologize i didn't tell you sooner. i just felt like you hated me so much that you would never give me a chance."

"well what about asa, he's still in high school, you can still build a relationship for him, its not to late for him."

"we have had a relationship for years ayden, he told me he didn't talk to you allot about me because every time you brought me up you got so angry and told him to shut up."

"really?"

"we have talked once a week for about 4 years now."

"but he never mentioned anything to me about it."

"he didn't think you wanted to hear about it. he actually purchased me my favorite piece of art last year for fathers day."

"what was that?"

"an amazing black and white photograph from my favorite photographer ... ayden kosacov."

as i sit here out on the deck of the hospital's psychological wing i realize that it has been so long since i have looked at stars. sure i've glanced, maybe even commented on seeing the big dipper to a nearby patron, but never have i just stared at each and every one of them with such tenacity. maybe i never had the time, maybe i never made time. each time i look at them i wonder deeper and deeper into space, sit in awe of how infinite it is. i seem so small when i get lost in nature. my problems seem so small when i am lost like this. we live in such a huge universe, and the moon itself has stared and watched mankind throughout the ages. if the moon could talk i wonder if it would scream at us, or just laugh.

(the title track transatlantic by death cab for cutie, just seems so fitting tonight to repeat in my head.)

i feel new. relieved. this is a new year. i view life a little more as a venture and less like a hassle. sure im scared of what's next, but i know there is more out there than what i have seen.

staring upward for an elongated period of time causes my mind to wonder on the reasoning of life, why are we here? how did we get here?

i once read that if the earth was a few degrees one way or the other on our axis we would either burn or freeze. how perfectly placed it seems we are. einstein even said that just by the examining the human eye he knew there was a God. but what about God now? the reason i believed when i was young was because religion was a psuedo-social club to me. cookies and juice, youth camps, after service get togethers. then my dad left, and my faith shrunk consequently. then i pursued a life of sex, drugs, and rock and roll, and somewhere in that equation God just doesn't fit. selfishly.

so what reasoning did i give myself to give up on God? now that i reflect upon my life i see that the only reason i didn't want to believe was simply because i didn't want the obligation to morality. i wanted a license to do what i wanted, when i wanted. and that's why i became agnostic. the logic was; because i want to screw everyone, and smoke anything there is no God. that makes no sense now. here. here a lot of things are placed in perspective on their own.

i need to rethink a lot of things in life. this being one of them. in the distance the wind slowly echoed my thoughts as it wrestled with the nearby trees. thanks God.

thanks for not going to far out of reach.

NEW CHAPTER
in certain light, in these moments, salvation has ambrosial lips

"hey, do you want to come inside, i mean the hard wood deck floor looks inviting and all but ..."

"oh wow, is that you nico?, i must have fallen asleep."

"yea, i would have let you stay out here, but its getting pretty cold."

"hey thanks." i said, half dreamt and half awake.

"busy day? i didn't see you around much at all."

"well, honestly my father came back from the dead, and God moved a tree over there."

"yea, sounds like a busy day ... what meds do they have you on?"

"no, its not like that at all."

"ayden, what are you going to do after this?"

"i have no idea, and maybe that's the best way to be."

"what do you mean?"

"well i have no plans, i have no goals. i am empty. but i do have trust. and i'm alive. and that's what matters, i am alive, and i want to be."

"what changed?"

"me. that's what i am trying to change. my outlook, my family. the fact that its a big world out there, and i know that, and even though i am scared, i'm willing to go take it over."

"who are you? you don't sound like the ayden i met a couple of weeks ago."

"im not."

we both pause, not an awkward silence, just a pause. almost to take in this whole night and our conversation. to be honest i think when you can sit in moments of silence with someone you are at a certain depth in a relationship; silent, still, and the absence of the need to speak and yet absolutely comfortable.

"ayden, what were your dreams when you were a kid?"

"well ... i think i wanted to be a transformer more than anything else. but after i realized i could not change into a giant metal dinosaur i think i wanted to

93

be a photographer, but that was years later. its the only thing in my life that made me feel, somewhat serene and in my element. but now i don't know, maybe i need to settle down and get a real job like my brother. make some money, get a nice place of my own."

"really? but why? what does money have to do with anything?"

"it's that money makes life easier, it gives life a sense of stability. with all the grown ups and downs i just think a normal job will just give me security, and that's what i think i want right now."

"ayden, how long do you think that's going to last? you say that is what you want, but that's not what you need. sure, for the first little while you can love what money can accumulate, but at the end of the day it can't buy contentment, only comfort."

"but where is photography going to get me?"

"anywhere you want. don't you ever listen to yourself? you said that photography makes you feel serene, in everyone's life there is something that makes each of us come alive. in our element as you put it. for you its photography. and if you give up on it it will slowly end up choking you on the inside."

"but money seems to solve so many problems for so many people."

"that's what you think, but after the amenity wears off you realize that what money can by are only 'things'. and 'things' are lost, begin to fade, decompose, and when the furor is over—discarded."

"but no one seems to care about my photography."

"who are you trying to appease? everyone else? why do you care what others think, especially people you don't know? you need to do what makes you come alive. and when others see your ardor, the entire world will concede to your passion."

"but what about financial security. what about stability, what about the very thing the world seems to be searching after!"

"answer me this ayden. on your death bed, when all is said and done. when every memory in your life has already been made. as your heart rate and breathing begins to crawl, who do you want to be holding you? do you want it to be your two story house, white picket fence, jaguar, or your bank account statement? or do you want it to be those you loved throughout your life, and those who love you. there is so much more to life than money, there is passion."

"i want ..."

then the door to the deck opened and a brut of nurse stormed out.

"is anyone out here?"

and then nico turned to me and whispered

"you cant tell him out here, im supposed to be in my room."

"uhhh, just me sir. we were ... i accidentally fell asleep im sorry."

"all right get back inside, this cant happen again or we start taking away your outdoor privileges, you got it?"

"yes sir, im sorry, it wont happen again."

but as i was walking in, i wanted so badly to go back out there and hide with her. i wanted to grasp her and tell her that @ the end of my life, on my death bed, i knew exactly what i wanted i wanted to hold. or rather i thought i knew who.

that night as i laid in my bed i wondered if this is what the prelude to love felt like. the constant thoughts running through my head, but all have added her into the equation. her coruscating eyes, her messy hair basking about her neck. her transparency. even when she raised her voice to make a point i just wanted to lock my arms around her waist and hold her, kissing whatever skin was exposed. she was surreal,

she felt like grace.

she embodied mercy.

i wanted her

... to be my salvation.

NEW CHAPTER
an ending and a countdown …

i have kept a journal for years now, well off and on really. ok, well more off than on. i actually started because my dad told me about this friend he had in college who would write 2 science fiction stories every morning when he would wake up just to practice writing, and these were not short stories either; these were like full on character development, action, isaac asimo-vish stories. it inspired me so i began to write two poems every night. years later i went back and read them and dear god, they are the most horrible pieces of literature ever written. more like a haiku on crack rock than a inspirational rune.

none the less the incognizable scratching turned into a journal that i've tried to keep since then. i have started back up these last few days. i scratch out random thoughts or a drawing now and again. i think writing in a journal is important, if we would only learn from ours (and others) failures we wouldn't suffer/struggle so much in life.

when i first began writing in my journal i would never write the date, i don't know if i was afraid of time or just wanted nothing to do with it. i think i wanted it to be like steve mcqueen or johnny cash … timeless.

now i notice time; i take account of every second of it. whether it flies or slows, whether it is good to me, or if it is healing any sort of wound in which only it could heal. i write the date, the second, the year, and exactly where i am in every journal entry. as if life has a GPS system i figure when watching my whole life on beta in the afterlife i can recap those minutes rather quickly and skip to the good stuff like skydiving, that crazy night @ the cha cha, or (while pushing slow motion on the vcr) rooftop conversations with a bottle of wine with good company.

nico. i think this women is contagious though. i think now i could be diagnosed with insanity, because every thought seems to begin and end with her.

"i leave today." the green eyed girl said.
"what????"

"ayden, my time here is done, im checking myself out."

"you can do that?"

"well i checked myself in, with the agreement that i can check myself out any-time after two weeks. my time here is up, i cant help anymore here, and i don't think i can be helped anymore than i already have."

but what was i supposed to do, ask her to stay in a mental hospital for me? how do i tell her that she was the best therapy for me.

she was my medication.

she was my sanity.

"ok nico, goodbye."

"ok ayden, you take care of yourself."

"keep your chin up."

"what?"

"nothing, never mind."

she turned back down the hall towards her room and i knew the only place to go was to my room, and like awake thinking for the next couple weeks of what i should have said as she walked away.

"WAIT!"i said as she turned around knowing i didn't have anything to say.

"i need to see you again, i mean when i get out of this place, ill want to see you again. catch up. talk"

"ayden, you do not need anyone, you need to find all that you can about your-self before you search out those around you."

"i know, and i will, and i have. but i can't let you just walk out of here, and out of my life forever. please just give me your address. so i can at least write you a letter or something."

"but then you will have my address, and your crazy," she said with a smirk, "in case you haven't noticed your a patient in an mental ward."

"but i need to stalk you while you sleep." i said with the same smirk.

"see i told you were witty somewhere deep down. ok here is the deal. you said you were a photographer right?"

"right, and ..."

"well have you ever done any art or gallery shows?"

"well yes, one." and then i contemplated about telling her about the one piece i sold ... to my brother, who gave to my father without me knowing.

but ... "there pretty hard to set up, but i've entered a local gallery show in the past."

"fair enough, so that was your first. then i will be at your 10th."

"what!!??"

"well, enter into 9 more shows and ill be at the tenth one."

"that is so many shows, plus how will you know how many shows i've done?"

"you may not know mine, but i know your real name. i guess you will just have to make sure they are well advertised."

"your insane, that is seriously a long time!"

"well its your call, enter 10 and you will see me again."

"wait, what? what is your real name?"

"ten"

"ten, your name is 'ten'?"

"no, your 10th show and ill tell you, i don't want you trying to look me up."

"fair enough."

"fair enough. goodbye ayden, seeing you soon is up to you, so for now a simple goodbye must do."

NEW CHAPTER
a 'roommate', direction,
and the miracle of resurrection

its been a week. a mere week later since she left my sight. my mind has floated from here and past, to there and now. my days are numb with a rabid intent for the future. im ready to be out. this is feeling less like a voluntary enrollment and more like a prison sentence. i want to find my way in the world, fight my way into the world and conquer it now. i want to create, absorb, interact.

i want

... her.

my mother and i have had a couple long talks. she weeps, she talks, she weeps, she talks. really im ok with it, i mean i feel somewhat deceived, but i understand they both had good intentions. plus i have a father back. sure we have lost some years but its like lazarus, or Jesus; he's back from the dead. he's even planned another "business trip" to come hang out with my brothers and i, i am sure they will run the gambit of emotions but in the end they will find lazarus and Jesus as well.

"ayden, your going home today." 'doc' said

"what?"

"well its time. your parents, and staff, and subsequently the court think that your ready to go home. i am sure the you will have some repercussions from the court, probably probation and mandatory sessions with a psychologist, but i think your ready ayden."

at that moment my throat tightened, and my stomach hit the floor. was i ready, was this it. have i learned enough.

"ok doc, let me go grab my stuff, it was great working with you, i appreciate the time and seeing in me things i couldn't see myself."

"hey mom, how life." i said as i literally bounded into her idling car that was parked right outside the front doors.

99

"good, son, and yours?" she seemed caught off guard.

"amazing! life is … good."

"well, that's good to hear … umm … son"

"yea mom?"

"what meds do they have you on."

"(i laugh a little and then attempt to clear my throat) nothing mom, they try to ween you off everything by the time you leave. i'm good mom, i am definitely sober."

"its just that i haven't seen you smile in, well in years now son."

"i don't know what it is mom, i feel free, and really i am just excited to get some real food. like a nice greasy burger or something. and what about a coffee too?"

"sounds good to me, lets go."

that afternoon it felt like me and my mom had talked for real for the first time in my entire lives. no more were we mother and son, but we were coequal adults, maybe even friends. talking about real matters. from politics to recent movies; from dad to our mutual utter hatred of mayonnaise.

i felt like we connected in a totally different way. its funny how honesty can break down a world of communicational barriers.

we had dinner as a family that night. my mother, my brothers and i. @ first they were so scared, or nervous to even look at me. but right when they got there my mom and i were already sitting down|@ the dinner table and i started drooling, and my mom pretended for some reason that i was hard of hearing and was yelling.

"DO YOU WANT PEES WITH YOUR MASHED POTATOES?"

and i would slur my words and scream back,

"MANKS MOM, I LUB YOUR PEES PLEES."

then me and my mom started cracking up.

at first my brothers didn't get the humor but after a few seconds they both started laughing. asa ended up on the floor, and my older brother even slapped me on the back of the head, just like when we were kids. we ended up hugging, and laughing.

after that the night was pretty great. sure i couldn't tell them about mom and dad, but it was cool to tell them all the stories about what is was like on the "inside."

they thought 'gerrymander' lady was the best, and i agreed. we talked about what was next and what i was going to do. they told me how the bauhaus called and even sent a small patch of flowers thinking i was dead. and for all they know they can think i'm dead cause i'm never going back to that place. i read the card though, jenn-iveve even signed it with her usual little heart right above the 'i'. how fitting.

i spent the next week just lounging around my mothers house. i moved back in because not only was it court recommended, but i needed to be back. near her, near asa. near people. near people actually living life. my stomach goes into spurts of pain, like a small razor, shaving my insides. but moments later it flees as if to remind me of that one fateful night. i count is as penance for my sin. the doctors can't figure out what it is, and each time they tell me to make sure i get plenty of rest and let them know when, or if, it ever happens again. it does.

i didn't get a job, not right away anyway. i talked to the admissions office at the local university, let loose my sob story of overcoming depression and such and they let me in. i think the deciding factor was when i told them that i was going to major in psychology because the people at the hospital "really made a difference in my life, therefore i wanted to make a difference in someone else's life." well its somewhat true. i really liked doc. and he helped. i don't want to be a shrink by any means but hey, why not. i figure i have a leg up on everyone else.

when we take deviant psychology classes i wont even have to go on the 'field trips' ill have already been. and even if its a requirement ill score some points with the professor by knowing my way around.

im going to minor in photography. even masters like myself could use a couple hints here and there. plus i would love to have access to a dark room. i can suck up to the prof. and know when the next shows are taking place.

there is a new trend in my work. sure i still love taking pictures of decompositions, but now i like the cycle of decompositions. the birth, the growth, the life, and inevitably the death and rust.

the eventual orphaned anything.

i have been taking pictures of precisely everything. this winter has made this town especially photogenic. i even had the opportunity to cross the border into oregon and spend a weekend with my older brother @ mount hood. that place is amazing, and all the while he was skiing, or hitting on various snowboard instructors, i was taking pictures of everything in sight, black and white of course.

what i have i begun to do is make a series of four pictures in one frame, side by side. each picture being a little bigger than a postcard. it starts out with something young (like a little girl, or a budding plant, or a skyscraper in developmental stages, still being built). then the next picture switches to something a little older, then a little older, and ends with either an elderly person, or a burnt down house, or even in one i had a close up of a bucket of rusty railroad spikes i personally thought was incredible.

so for example in one of my pieces i called 'careless, the amateur youth' the sequence would be a young girl playing in puddles out in the rain with a broken umbrella, wearing her mothers heels. then the second picture would be a house that was almost finished in completion, then third a flower that was just starting to droop, then finally a picture of an old man in the back of the car, holding an umbrella looking out the back window, and ominously in the reflection you can see that they are driving past (or through) a cemetery. i've called the entire display appropriately 'encircle.' and for once in my life i'm proud of something i've done.

i've signed up for my first three shows. all with months in between them. at this rate it literally could be another 2 years before i see 'her' again. regardless i have amazing motivation at this point, and its not just her, its that it feels like life is renewed.

astonishing motivation.

the next few weeks were spent preparing for, and worrying about university. new years eve meant nothing to me this year because i had already had my new years two months prior in a near padded room, where vows of a fresh start were flung rabidly around the room. now with school starting, and a countdown to a show coming up, things looked, well ... rather promising.

NEW CHAPTER

january 16th, im so bloody nervous. schools been exorbitant. i mean really good. whatever. my mind is everywhere today, much like old times. i woke up with the sunrise and relentlessly sleep has evaded me these past couple nights. not only do i have a test in two of my subjects tomorrow, but my first art show is tonight.

secretly i am anticipating that 'she' is just merely exaggerating about 10 entire shows and just shows up to the first one, in slow motion of course. i don't know who i am keeping this secretive from. maybe just myself. she will be wearing a black dress, with a beige scarf, (which she will inevitably drop by the end of the night) she will be so gorgeous, basked in her natural beauty (barely any makeup, the way i have always liked girls). we will talk and i will make her laugh. we will talk about memories shared and hold each other close, not letting go of any article of clothing or at least touching somewhere, anywhere, on each other's person all night. i will magically lose a couple pounds and gain a couple points of iq if even just for tonight.

she will whisk out of the door and her scarf will fall. i will be the one to discover it, and as right before she walks back through the door i will be cleaning up what's left of my art show ... *where i will have sold all but one of the pieces, which i hold back for art's sake. so as she strolls wondering back into the gallery door we will be suddenly alone. 'the blowers daughter' by damien rice instantaneously comes on onto the auditorium speakers and we begin to slow dance.

the camera fades to the left and when it pans back to the right were at the alter, my brothers are my best men and some other really handsome guys, who i met in college apparently, are there also as groomsmen. she is beautiful, we skip to the part of "i do's" and then the credits begin to roll, still playing 'the blowers daughter', but right before they do it says "... and they lived happily ever after."

something like this.

or not.

the gallery show was amazing. though i felt totally out of place as far as what i wore. it was at a local gallery and one of the two requirements of the show was that we had to donate 10% of our profits from the show to a charity of our choice. i was fine with that because 10% of $0.00 is 0.00 so what did i have to lose? the other requirement was to respect that this was a black tie affair. honestly, no one told me. so by the end of the night i think that everyone thought that i knew it was a black tie affair but i was an euro-trash 'artist' (please say 'artist' with a french accent).

i wore my typical taut blue jeans, broken social scene t-shirt, and finding out it was a black tie affair after i got there i threw on a suit jacket that i found on the floorboard of my little brothers car. yes artist'. now all i needed was a beret and some absinth and this night would have been complete.

the show went amazing, i cant even describe it in full! what had happened was that some local guy thought he would set up a gallery show for charity. he charged people 25$ just to get in the door, free wine was served of course (something i DEFINITELY strayed away from). i think the fact 'proceeds are donated to charity' probably scared a lot of local artists away, but still there must have been 30 of us with displays. the fortunate thing for me is that i was the only artist who was under the age of 35, which attracted everyone who was under 35 to come talk to me, which attracted the older men, which attracted their 'charitable' wives.

the other advantage is that the other artists seriously sucked. i mean i am by no means cocky, but good Lord these people sucked. one person did this collage of different fruits. let me explain. its worth it.

see he would take pictures of fruit and then cut them out and paste them on to canvas. i really should have loaned him some catchy slogans to fling underneath and he would have sold a couple. but no, they were just fruit. no lie, if i had a kid sister she could have done better.

then this other lady had paintings of farm animals, all sorts, and she would take this metal fencing stuff and wrap the entire frame as if the animals were fenced in. creative, but if you were not into country/southern style interior decorating then this wasn't for you.

so in other words i was some sort of local interest. i mean come on, here i am, an x-psycho, still healing from wounds from a self inflicted gun shot, taking pictures of the evolutionary sequence of our lives. i am laughably the most insensate genius at this event.

i sold 3 of my 12 pieces. and the funny thing is that i was thinking that i wasn't going to sell any of them so i marked the prices so high, the highest selling for $110.00. after the contribution to world vision, the organization i picked to donate my money to i had made $230.oo.

the other astonishing happenstance was that all the press that appeared @ the show, to seem as though they were somewhat benevolent, loomed around my display. i even received invitations to do interviews for the local papers, including the seattle weekly, but not the stranger unfortunately. life is good.

at the end of the night when i had shook the last hand, and packaged the last of my photographs up to put in my brothers car, it wasn't the notoriety, the money, or even the sip of free wine that made it worth it. it was the fact i had 2 shows down 8 to go.

after the show i sat at the empty pike place market to write in my journal and simply just watch the random person pass by in a lackadaisical strut. in search of a unsystematic vendor selling what was left of their flowers in brown wrapping, or just a trip downtown to feel like they have done something with their lives today.

i wonder why we always feel the need to do something with our day. we can't sit back with a book at home and enjoy the peace, we have to constantly be moving, going, doing, achieving, just so when we lie upon our pillow we don't feel useless and unresolved. what an oxymoron i am, here i am scolding the neo-yuppies for wine shopping when i myself could not sit alone @ home in peace, but instead came here and immediately began to judge others, i don't want to do that anymore. i want to start taking my own advice and stop forcing them on others, simply let it be.

i think ill buy some flowers in brown wrapping.

NEW CHAPTER
basic principles of debating kierekgard's theory of the relodiagnosisology

why is this world resound with so much bitterness? do we as westerner's really have it that bad? why do people emphasize the negative or pessimistic outlook of this one chance life rather than the good. maybe i am naive, maybe this world is truly out to get me and everyone is born a criminal. dark alley's look to me as great opportunities for a black and white photo, not a noun i must avoid in fear.

i am reminded of a song that would not make it on the radio in the timeframe of his current state of unrest. it was by a man named louis armstrong, who did not know the same respect and freedoms as his musical counterparts today. instead of writing about the familiarities that surrounded him, like oppression or racism, he sang a song called "(what) a wonderful world". listening to the current radio you would think hate and violence governs entire genres.

i choose to believe the best in people now.

my mother once told me a story of two young boys which set me on my path for optimism. the boys were between the ages of 10 and 12. the parents of these two boys set out to give each boy a Christmas contrary to their personalities and see how they would respond.

on christmas morning they woke the children up from the living room floor and told the boys to go to their rooms where their presents awaited them. the first boy was given every new toy imaginable. stacks and stacks of brand new games and packages were all his. as the parents walked in the room they saw the boy with toys lying on the floor crying. "what's wrong son?" asked the parents.

"all these toys will one day break and will be thrown away," the boy said.

the parents went into their other sons room where instead of presents there was huge mounds of manure. the entire room had a stench that crept now throughout the house. the boy, whose room was filled with manure, was not crying or upset but instead was frantically digging with a shovel.

"what are you doing son?" the dad asked.

"well dad, if there's this much manure there has to be a horse somewhere!"

sure the story is a bit juvenile but that's what i was when they told me the story. the point is that life is all in your outlook and attitude.

though i am trying to have a different outlook on life, the next few shows seemed years apart. i couldn't take it, time seemed to literally leisurely crawl. it seemed my entire childhood flew by slower. each year melding into the next. my life, like a continual amalgamation. studies were beneficial, and due to my psychology classes i have found that i appreciate learning and reading.

my father came to town. he actually saw one of my shows. i didn't know this but he was an artist much the same as i. upon learning that he could not paint or draw he turned to stain glass for a short stint. he said he had not kept any of his masterpieces because they looked 'better-n-pieces' he said. i see where i got my whit from. unfortunately.

my brothers took the news about the truth pretty hard, my older brother even thought he was lying until when he went to my mothers house. she was just standing over the kitchen counter making dinner with tears rolling down both cheeks. nothing else was said that night. we all feel betrayed, but we were adults now. i think that all our relationships are going to strengthen from here on out, they have to; honesty and time have a way of medicating even the deepest of hurts. i think asa has known for awhile. either that or he is a lot more stoic than i had ever anticipated.

i have received a little media exposure and believe people come and view my pictures simply because they saw my picture in the paper and not because they actually like my work in photography. my mother even clips out anything she sees in the paper with my name or picture on it. she makes it seem that she is genuinely interested in my art but i know how she really feels. she just likes the notoriety, and im sure its a good change of interpersonal communication @ work.

the only reason that i am glad that i am in the papers is because hopefully 'she' sees them also. the disadvantage to being in the papers for photography is that my professor and the other students @ university critique every single project i turn in. one or two people come and say something nice but i think everyone else is thinking that they could do so much better, or think that they would have used a different subject, or that my pictures all look the same, or are to dark or to bright. and they are probably right.

hey i didn't ask for notoriety, anyone can shoot themselves and then push a button to take a picture.

-ring ring
-ring ring

"hello, is ayden kosacov available?"

"this is him." i said trying to sound professional,

"hello ayden this is juliana from the portland museum of art."

"hello juliana, what can i do for you?"

"well were holding a three day show here in early march and we were calling regional artist from the area to see if they were interested in presenting their participate, would you be willing to display some of your works?"

"well of course, do i need to drive them down, or do you want them shipped?"

"if you can not make it to the show yourself we can pay for them to get shipped."

"no, its fine, ill come. i've never done a show in portland, it would be a great holiday."

"that's great, so … how long have you been interested in photography?"

"for years now, but i have only been proficient @ it for about 3 days now."

"no, ayden i've seen some of your stuff, its really good. i honestly think some of photography is mindless. i mean honestly i love black and white just as much as the next girl, but anyone can take a picture of a naked subject next to a tree and call it art. i like your stuff because it seems there is a sense of philosophy behind it."

"thanks so much, really i don't really like to think life can be captured with just black and white, but at least i can take snapshots of chapters i believe everyone will go through someday."

"i am sorry to sound like such a fan but really, was the little girl playing with her mothers hair at that coffee shop staged?"

"no, i was in there just toiling @ the coffee shop, i never intended to be out shooting that day, it just happened. the amazing thing is that the mother was upset at the little girl, as if she were a distraction. to be honest it made me want kids for the first time in my life."

"really? you never wanted kids before that day?"

"no i saw them more as a hassle, used only to pass down a last name and continue some drawing of a tree in an old bible. but now i see them as little futures, little mirrors of what you were, and are. i think allot of why i never wanted kids is because i thought i may screw up their lives, it was more out of fear of failure than my initial inconvenience theory."

"yea, my mother left us when i was young, and kind of the opposite happened. i wanted 14 kids just to prove to her and myself that i could do it. she saw me as an inconvenience and just, left. my father and i made it, but now i have a vendetta and i am out to start an orphanage with whomever i marry."

"well you might not want to tell him that till after your married."

"yes, well i'll keep my secret vendetta under wraps till its to late for him to back out. thanks for the advise."

"so tell me how did you get involved with the museum?"

"my father, he has been in the art scene pretty heavy for years now and i needed a summer job between semesters a couple years ago, i never left. now i set up shows and help with tours when it gets busy, which is rare, but still."

"are you still going to school?"

"nope, i've finished my AA but what does that do?"

"i know right?"

"honestly i have no idea what i want to do with my life, so i just dropped out instead of going through another 2 years of college and never finishing. i figure college will be here for the rest of my life, so i might as well go and find what i love and pursue it, then pursue a piece of paper that says 'you've graduated' and it be meaning less and leave me stranded in a job for the rest of my life that im miserable @."

"what a great place in life to be @."

"yea right ayden. you mean sitting here in the same place trying to figure out what i want to do with the rest of my life?"

"your not lost, your not lost @ all, you know exactly what your doing."

"and what exactly am i doing"

"searching the world over, looking for nothing more than yourself. you have to trust, trust that life is going to come along side of where you are and help you out. stop worrying so much about tomorrow and live out all you can today. i think people have bought into some underlying thought that you have to have graduated high school by age 18, college by 22, then you have to be married by 25, then have your first kid by 29, your first house by 32, partner @ 40, et cetra, but i want to find out who made these social rules and break his knee caps. i think so many people rush to play by social rules that they neglect the fact that you can make your own rules!"

"wow ... so tell me, how do you really feel?"

"im sorry, its just all this has been on my mind."

"no i love it, insight from someone like you is invaluable because i know you have put some thought behind it and arrant just blabbing to try to impress me."

"what do you mean?"

"well, its just, well no offense, but men in general. they will try to say something profound, have memorized a couple random quotes, just to prove that they are this profound thinker, and that's just to take you back to their place, when in all reality they sound like a fumbling baboon."

"and you have had encounters with such creatures?"

"really i have, i once met this boy, and we got pretty serious, and i took him out to dinner to meet my father. the guy started talking all this psuedo-intelligent slang around and it sounded all so familiar, he just kept repeating what he had said to me and every other person he met. and now he was saying it to my dad. turned out that he had just taken 3 or 4 paragraphs from kierekgard and memorized them. he wasn't intellectual @ all, he just knew a memorized schpeel and seemed to impress every blonde bimbo he came across."

"well it worked on you for awhile."

"well i wised up fast, im not to keen on personalities that are more memorization techniques than true self. if you love it then love it, if you hate it just say so. any time you fake something you like or hate just to win approval i think you should have, as you put it, have your knees broken."

"very true, very true."

(lull)

"ok, well it was nice talking to you ayden. im sorry to take up so much of your time."

"no worries @ all, i was just sitting around here debating kierekgard's theory of the relodiagnosisology."

"wow, sounds impressive, i didn't even know that was a word!"

"that's because your iq quadfudells yours."

"yes that to."

"all right juliana, ill talk to you later."

"goodbye."

as i sat there for a few moments i had to sit back and count my blessings. life is good. i was high on my new found admiration and others interests in my life. no one seemed to care about my life until i tried to kill myself. but that didn't seem right. it wasn't the act of a bullet in my side that attracted attention at all, i think it is because i overcame emotions that everyone in life feels and i just happen to beat failure.

in my required history class at uni we learned abraham lincoln lost every election and finally decided one day just to run for president and won. who does that? who just gets beat up on their whole lives then thinks that they can accomplish the impossible. i guess that is what sets success stories from statistics.

i am not saying that i am a success story now just because i took a couple of pictures, but what i am saying is that i could have been just another suicide statistic and instead am accomplishing where i only saw failure in the past. and what is failure? life has taught me in the last couple of months that there should be a different word for the first time you fail. it should be called "falter". because everyone falters, but failure is when you screw up, and do not learn from your mistakes, then you keep making the same wrong decision over and over.

that is failure; simply not learning from previous mistakes. make no mistake! we all falter, i thought i was the only one who felt like this but soon realized that we all feel alone in our impropriety's. we are an army of lonely and tired souls. some willing to change, others content when they finally concede to failure.

and then it hit me. pain like none other i had experienced in life. like another bullet in my side, like 2 inch thorns are pulled slowly through my intestines. pain impaled me and i flung the phone off the counter and buckled to my knees. i heard my heart beat for only the second time in my life, and i finally could empathize with every heart attack story i had ever heard. i want to die, just get this over with, someone pull a trigger, anything to stop the pain ...

CONCLUSION

at first i could ignore the constant beep of the machine to my side, but as of late it reminds me of the chinese water torture. i am not naive to the fact that i am dying, i know the signs and all but the absence of my breath contends that i am still alive. i feel i have lived a worthwhile life at this point. sure, i have regrets but who, except maybe Jesus, could say they do not. i have learned so much, i believe its easier to appreciate life when death seems so very close. but i am surrounded with what means the most to me now, my family. someone once mentioned to me that "if it doesn't breath, it doesn't matter." i think he or she had life figured out quite well, and well before me.

there are two regrets worth telling of as i look back upon my existence. the first would be that i would have loved to spend more time with those i loved. i think this is a common regret but no matter how much people warned me and i took heed i still wish i could have spent every waking moment with them somehow.

the second regret would be the mystery that is nico. i have not heard from 'her' since my days in the psychological wing of the hospital, but i realize why now. its not that she was an illusion created in my mind, or some sort of collapsed mental episode, but that she needed to leave me on my own. she saw that i needed to grasp onto something, and she didn't want it to be her; she wanted it to be life itself. i see now i simply needed a face to put with the new realized faith in myself.

it didn't hurt. somewhere deep down i knew that i had fallen more for what she taught me, then what the future could hold between us. its not that i regret finding her and falling romantically into her, but that i never got to thank her for teaching me how to breath.

some days i think i see her and it appears as though she has not aged a day, even though it has been some time since i have seen her. other times i almost feel her watching me, maybe she is, maybe she is not. but it is reassuring to think that someone out there wants you to succeed along side of you. a silent partner. an angel giver. an unseen companion.

i found love how i thought it to be ... a sleep deprivating pain in my chest that is only filled when that voice rings through your ear, touches your hand, or slows down to catch a red light so you can have one more second in each others eyes, and lips. and i have been so graced to know this love for many, many years now.

there are no plaques or awards of me anywhere and never will be. the picture's i took are soon to be taken out of the frames and replaced with a better photographer, or maybe just a more creative. i never won many alkaloids, nothing i can recall of importance. the job's i took have since replaced me. and yet my life achievements could never be available on a incidental paper anyway. i realize now that no conquests or acquisitions matter in the grand scheme of life.

it took me all these year's to finally figure this out, and now that i am 76 year's old they must sound like the ramblings of an old man. the attempt on my own life with a simple gun seems ages ago, the only remains are lessons learned, and two circular scars a couple inches apart.

old age is taking my life now, my breath is slowing, my eyesight is fading. but i have lived life. the money i have made is not here by my bedside, neither any of the possessions that a man can aquire.

what is here is not a what at all, but the who. my beautiful bride juliana, whom i met at a art show she had set up in portland. and my two beautiful children who now have children of their own. if i should pass tonight family please remember that life is good. regardless of circumstances, regardless of oppression or depression, regardless of what might happen tomorrow, or what happened last night, or what will happen tonight....

life is good.

the orphaned soundtrack: (songs to read the book to)

doves-some cities-black and white town
the stills-logic will break your heart-gender bombs
death cab for cutie-transatlantism-transatlantism
rogue wave-descended vultures-loves lost guarantee
sigur ros-hvarf/heim disc 2-staralfur
damien rice-9-blowers daughter
innocence mission-we walked in song-happy birthday
rachel's-music for egon schiele-family portrait
bloc party-weekend in the city-kreuzberg
animal collective-feels-did you see the words
code seven-dancing echoes-roped and tied
blonde redhead-misery is a butterfly-elephant woman
the sea and cake-the fawn-sporting life
fiest-the reminder-brandy alexander
radiohead-in rainbows-videotape
ryan adams—easy tiger-two
nico-these days

978-0-595-47856-9
0-595-47856-5

Made in the USA
Lexington, KY
29 October 2013